The Final Cipher

A heart-pounding thriller and conclusion about power, privacy, and the price of choice in a connected world (The Last Message Trilogy Book 3)

Stephen Bentley

Contents

INTRODUCTION

No inspiration was required for me to put metaphorical pen to paper to write this trilogy. However after I had completed the trilogy, I did find this quote attributed to the late Stephen Hawking about the use of AI which I found of interest, and I hope you do too:

Hawking's comment to the BBC in 2014 that AI could "spell the end of the human race" was in response to a question about potentially revamping the voice technology he relied on. He told the BBC that very basic forms of AI had already proven powerful but creating systems that rival human intelligence or surpass it could be disastrous for the human race.

He may proved to be right but I wonder if certain Presidents could be more disastrous for the human race than artificial intelligence.

What is potentially more dangerous? Human intelligence wrongly applied or for the wrong reasons, or artificial intelligence applied benignly?

That is food for thought but this isn't: please read the trilogy in order starting with *The Last Message*.

Chapter One: The Final Cipher

Six months is a long time to stay underground.

Long enough to change your name, your hair, and your habits. Long enough to disappear from the public eye and slip into the digital underworld. Long enough, Maya Dalton had discovered, to learn how to break into systems that were never meant to be opened.

Her fingertips hover above the keyboard in the dim light of her London flat, the hum of her custom-built rig the only sound in the room. Outside, the city is its usual restless self—sirens, laughter, the occasional burst of music—but inside, Maya is somewhere else entirely. Deep in a server farm in Geneva, threading her way through encrypted firewalls, chasing a rumour that refused to die.

Lionel Gage was dead. Or so they said.

She didn't buy it. Gage isn't the kind of man who vanishes quietly. When he disappeared after the collapse of the VEGA program, it felt too clean. Too final. A man like him didn't just *stop*.

And now, there are whispers—buried in darknet chatrooms, encoded in obscure research logs—of something else—a continuation, or maybe a mutation, of VEGA. And one name keeps appearing, like a glitch in the system: Dr Susan Voss.

Maya leans back in her chair, the glow of the monitors painting her face in cold light. She hadn't seen Felix Carter in nearly a decade—not since they'd both scraped through their journalism degrees at South Thames Poly. Back then, he was more interested in breaking code than breaking stories. Now, he is the reason she can do both.

He'd taught her the language of rootkits and zero-days, of exploits and shadows. She'd taught herself the rest—the obsession, the discipline, the paranoia.

Because this isn't just another story.

This is personal.

IT HAS BEEN SIX months to the day since she's heard or seen Alex. The clock burns past midnight in Maya's flat. London rain chatters against the window. The neon from the betting shop paints the room in blues and reds. She's alone. Again. She clicks through files on her laptop, chasing leads, racing some invisible deadline. Then, the sound—soft and calculated. Something sliding under her door. A brown envelope, anonymous. Maya stares at it, a drawn breath, then she's up. She tears it open. Inside, a thumb drive stamped with "THE FINAL CIPHER." Her heart skitters.

She reaches for the burner phone with a simple text to Alex.

Coordinates. Time.

No hesitation. Her laptop snaps shut. Her heart thrums like a live wire. Six months without contact, and now this. She swipes her desk clean, moves like a shadow. Slips the drive into her pocket and leans against the door. Listens. Silence but for the rain.

She packs quickly, the bag slung over her shoulder. In the glow of neon and darkness, she stands still, calculating, watching for movement in the night. She grabs a coat and heads into the hall. Pauses. A quick glance down the stairwell before she takes the stairs two at a time, quiet, controlled.

Outside, the world smells of wet pavement and diesel. She lingers near the doorway, eyes scanning. She crosses the street, keeping close to the buildings. Just another ghost in the rain.

A zigzag path. The narrow alleys wrap around her like a labyrinth, but she moves through them with confidence. An erratic line designed to lose anyone who might follow. She changes direction, hesitates, doubles back, vanishes into the maze again using all the tradecraft Alex taught her.

Fifteen minutes of this. The rain picks up, sheets now, covering her escape. She peels away from the main streets, into an industrial park. The sign says "Crown Imports." Abandoned but not empty. Her breath clouds in the night air as she moves.

A van sits parked, engine cold. She circles it once, checking the shadows, then slips inside.

Alex glances up, eyes sharp as ever. "Maya," he says, her name like a question and a statement. The van's interior is cluttered, chaotic in an organized way. Maps, surveillance gear, more electronics than a small office. Signs of a man off-grid.

Maya shivers from the rain, water pooling at her feet. She says nothing, just hands him the thumb drive, a silent explanation. It's stamped:

THE FINAL CIPHER

He takes it, holding her gaze. His hair is longer, and his clothes are worn but practical. A subtle transformation. "When did it arrive?"

She shrugs. "Hour ago." Her eyes scan the van, taking in the six months of distance and isolation. "Didn't know you were still in London."

Alex smirks, a ghost of the old him. "I'm not." He taps the drive. "This change anything?"

Maya hesitates, eyes flicking to his. "You tell me."

"Got a place we can check it?" The words come quick and sharp. Her voice, the same. Alex's nod is slight, his eyes already on the way ahead. "Follow me."

They leave the van and head to the roof of the abandoned warehouse. The wind is a living thing, pushing them, howling. Maya shivers as they climb. Alex moves with the confidence of a man who lives outside. Unburdened. Or careless. "You got it?" he asks, hand outstretched.

"Here." She gives him the drive. No hesitation. No touching. He plugs it into his laptop, screen flickering.

The rooftop is a wasteland of gravel and rust. Antennas reach into the sky like broken fingers. The city's lights are distant and dim, a reminder of how far they've drifted. Maya watches him, taking in the changes. Longer hair. Stubble. Worn clothes, sleeves cut away, running shoes tied and ready for anything. He's different. And the same.

Alex doesn't miss a beat. "Haven't seen you in months."

"Not for lack of trying."

He nods, the wind snatching the gesture. "Thought you'd move on."

"Not when there's a lead."

Her voice is determined, a hint of something else under it. He glances at her, measuring, then sets up the laptop. The screen bursts to life, bright against the night. The wind seems to pause as they both look at it.

A flicker. Lines of code, running fast. Alex's eyes widen. One word, tight and flat: "Nightfall."

Maya leans in, closer than she should be. "Again?"

"Maybe." His voice is low, caught between the gusts. "Who knows with secret programs that are blacker than black. You remember MI5 ran it?"

"Yeah, you."

"Yeah. Trained me, used me." He swallows, hard. "Then buried me."

The words hang between them, heavy as concrete. She steps back, crossing her arms, the cold finally catching her. But her eyes stay locked on his. "You're sure?"

He points at the screen, the cryptic dance of code. "No doubt. This is it."

She wants to know more, but his face says enough. Her mind races with the implications, the angles. He closes the laptop, breaks the spell. The wind surges, howling again, demanding their attention.

They stand apart, their bodies betraying what their words won't acknowledge. Hands brush as she takes back the drive. A moment too long. Eyes meet. She holds her breath, watches him. Waits for him to say it.

Alex breaks the silence. "Who sent it?"

Maya shakes her head. "No idea."

"Someone knew how to find you."

"Someone knew how to find *you*," she echoes, voice steady. She steps closer, not letting the distance grow. "It means something, Alex. Nightfall, this drive. It's a warning."

He absorbs the words, nodding slow, deliberate. "A threat."

Her voice is stronger, pushing against the wind. "Or an opportunity."

They face each other, the world beyond the rooftop forgotten. He sees the old determination, the old fire. She sees the same in him. They stand in the open, exposed, like the first time they met. Different and the same.

A beat too long.

Their world narrows to the glow of the laptop screen. The wind picks up, forcing them closer, touching. Not just their shoulders. Alex points out cryptographic signatures, his breath visible, mingling with hers in the cold air. She watches his intensity, clipped words matching her quickening pulse. Nightfall. She shivers. Gage. She mentions the rumours.

"Men like Gage don't just die," Alex says, his eyes locked on hers. "They transform." Their discussion spirals, words tumbling, charged with urgency and history. *Who sent the file? What does it mean?* The tension, like the wind, is a living thing.

The laptop screen flickers, the only light on the rooftop. Code spills out, fast and relentless. Alex traces patterns with his finger. "It's all here. Algorithms, techniques. Cryptographic signatures. Thought they buried this."

"They wanted you buried." Her voice carries both accusation and something softer. A challenge.

He hesitates, eyes on the screen. Then her. "It was dead. Supposedly dismantled years ago." He leans in, closer than he's been in months. The words low, fierce. "Why now?"

Maya's mind races. "To get your attention."

"Didn't work."

"It did." She meets his gaze, the distance evaporating.

"Gage," she says.

He stiffens, jaw tight. "What about him?"

"The rumours. His death. Everyone says—"

He interrupts her, "Like I said, men like Gage don't just die. They transform."

She watches him, gauging, knowing his distrust is as strong as ever. "This change your mind?"

The wind bites, cold and raw. They huddle closer, a reflex more than a decision. She points at the screen, at the spiralling lines of code. "This proves he's dead, Alex."

"Or alive and working." He cuts her off again, the words half frustration, half something else. "Men like Gage..."

"You sure he's still breathing?"

"Sure of nothing." His voice breaks, an old scar tearing open. He snaps the laptop shut. "I'm gone."

The cold pushes them together, tighter. The laptop's light, gone now, leaves them in shadow. Just breath, mingling.

Her hand, on his. "You're not."

"It's a trap."

"It's a story."

"It's suicide."

"It's us."

The truth between them, impossible to ignore. They've danced around it, denied it. But it's there, as relentless as the wind. A silence. A crack. It breaks.

"Okay," he says, a thousand layers in that single word. "Three days. Then I'm gone again."

A lie they both want to believe.

"Three days." She nods, not letting go. Of him. Of this.

And the city waits below, wide open, ready to consume them whole.

She moves to go, her steps reluctant. "See you in the morning."

"Five hours." He slips her a burner phone, just in case. "Don't disappear."

Maya takes it, and the wind, with a final push, drives her back to the maze of streets below.

Chapter Two: Ghosts of Nightfall

Night becomes day without ever getting light. The rain stays with them, a third partner in crime, pushing Maya to the safehouse where Alex is already working. They meet with words unspoken, and the six-month absence is washed away. Just like that. The Final Cipher spills its secrets on the main screen. Alex breaks encryption while Maya paces, his precision matching her energy. The cramped space forces them close; their past draws them closer. When the code reveals active protocols, their eyes lock.

The room is filled with the rhythmic tap of keys and the faint hum of machines. Shadows from the monitors stretch across blackout curtains and bare walls. The place is as stripped down as he is, utilitarian and packed with hardware. Servers stacked in corners, wires snaking across the floor. Maya's eyes trace the chaos. Different safehouse, same old Alex.

His voice breaks her thoughts, low and focused. "Ready?"

She nods. Her pace mirrors the racing of her heart.

Their world narrows to the contents of The Final Cipher. Data glows bright, ethereal in the dim space. He works fast, breaking through encryption layers. Algorithms crumble, one after another, under his assault. She circles him, barely contained energy, the closeness winding her tighter. His fingers fly, but he doesn't miss her movements. Their bodies brush, accidental and charged. Her breath catches. A triumphant look flashes across his face as another encryption yields. She leans over him, a coil springing. Heat from the chase, from him.

The code spills across the screen.

Alex points to a string of numbers, his words quick. "These are current." His eyes search hers. "Protocols from last week."

The news hits like a jolt, electric. "So, Nightfall never died," she breathes, her mouth near his ear.

"Worse," he says, grim, assured. "It evolved."

The code unspools in fragments, hinting at something deeper, darker. He watches her absorb the implications, her intensity and need to pursue. He knows it all too well. It pulls him in, a current he can't resist.

The cramped space, the old secrets. The past between them, raw and vivid.

The final decryption hits the screen.

Coordinates. Abandoned MI5 dead drop. East London.

Maya studies the details, a smile just out of reach. Her hand touches his shoulder, a grip, a question. She wants to go now. He feels her urgency and nods, already moving to prepare.

She has a bag of gear, packed and ready. Like always.

She paces the room, still racing the clock. Watching him, the pull between them fierce as it ever was. He checks his gun, smooth and practiced, tucking it into his waistband. A look, her, the gun, the open door. Calculated and intense.

"We need to move." His voice firm, definitive.

A shared breath. Then they're gone.

THE BUILDING YAWNS WIDE, hollow and ghostly, as they slip inside. Maya breathes in dust and damp, breathes out purpose. They cling to the shadows. Rain tracks their steps like a persistent detective. Windows cracked like old bones. Her flashlight arcs over silent workstations, the artefacts of a life before. Abandoned but not empty, she thinks again, both them and the building. Their footsteps are whispers in the dark. Her mind blazes. Strategy. Focus. A door—her heart skips—half-open. Another. Locked, then open. Hidden room. Files. Cards. She looks to Alex. He's already on it.

He digs through cabinets. Dust puffs into the air. Their names, redacted but unmistakable. She clutches them, shakes off the cobwebs. "Hargrove," she reads, fingers tracing the outline of the card. "Nightfall's logistics officer." Her pulse is loud in her ears. "He's still active?" The words, a challenge and a revelation. She watches Alex, his jaw a tight line of old betrayal.

They sift through it all. Cold records of a past refusing to stay buried. Outside, the wind howls and threatens. A noise, sudden and sharp, cuts through the abandoned halls. A pause. An understanding. They grab what they can and move. The rain, a curtain they dive behind, relentless in its pursuit.

THE CAR IS A safe haven. Barely. Maya tosses the files onto the seat, water still dripping from her coat. They stare at them, daring them to speak.

"Financials," Alex says, "private firms, offshore accounts." His eyes dart over the papers, his mind a machine, sorting and piecing together. He stops. Fingers on a page, silent as the blood pounding in her head.

Maya grabs the paper. Stares. "Alive," she says.

"Privatised." Alex's voice, low and intense. "Not buried."

"Then funded." Her breath a shiver, her hands, a vice.

They absorb the implications, the living weight of what they've found. The files stare back, more questions than answers. Alex starts the engine, the decision already made. It roars, and they're gone, rain and night swallowed up behind them.

THE PUB SLOUCHES IN Southwark like it's ready to fold into itself. Maya and Alex cross its threshold. The smell of regret and stale hops greets them like an old enemy. Low lights. Eyes behind pints of bitter. A place for men with pasts they can't shake. They spot him in a corner booth. Old MI5. A washed-out ghost. A husk. Hargrove sees them and flinches, but Alex closes in, words like ammunition. "The Final Cipher," is all he says.

The colour drains from Hargrove's face. "Bloody hell! You shouldn't have that," he mutters, his hands white-knuckled on his glass. He moves to stand.

"Sit down," Alex says, a command with no room for refusal. Maya slips in next to him, boxing him in. Hargrove's eyes dart, animal in a trap. He takes a long swallow of whisky. His hands still shake. "Nobody should have that. You don't know what you're messing with."

"Then tell us," Maya pushes, the old reporter's edge.

Hargrove sighs, a wheeze, too many cigarettes. He knows he has no choice. "It was never dismantled." His voice is rough and broken. "Privatised. Sold to the highest bidder." He leans in, sweat on his forehead. "With the government's blessing."

He waits for a reaction but gets none. Just their eyes glaring at him. Alex watches, calculating. Maya, with the intensity that scares lesser men.

"They've weaponised it." His voice is a rasp. "Surveillance is just the start. Algorithms don't just track behaviour now. They shape it."

The words hit hard. Maya's mind spins with implications. Alex absorbs it like a blow, then stands. "Who?" One word, full of command.

Hargrove hesitates, eyes twitching.

"Gage?" Alex asks, voice cold, sharp.

"Is it Gage?" Maya insists, her breath close to his face.

"He's gone," Hargrove whispers like a conspirator. "Gage has gone."

The old man's phone buzzes. He jerks like he's been shot. Reads the screen. Face drained, empty.

"They know you're here." His voice cracks. "You need to go. Now."

He slips a thumb drive into Alex's hand, the action barely perceptible. Before they can push more, Hargrove is up, stumbling to the back door, vanishing like he was never there.

The pub shifts. Eyes turning their way. Phone calls, whispers. Time to move. They're out the door, into the night, before the dust can settle.

Cold air and urgency. They dive into the car, drive already in the laptop, engine turning over. Rain pours down as the machine powers up. They're not sure if they were followed or not. Only sure they need to disappear.

They cut through streets, sharp and focused. The pub and its ghosts far behind, though the secrets cling to them still. Too close to call. It makes their pulse race, makes their blood thrum.

It makes them more alive than they've been in months.

THE NEW SAFEHOUSE IS a shell, empty and echoing around them. Alex and Maya, crouched over the glow of a laptop, track every keystroke like it might explode. The hours blur. Hargrove's drive spills secrets, but not fast enough. An avalanche of information. A code-cracked chorus. "Fuck," Alex mutters as he pushes it further, a mad conductor with too many instruments. Offshore accounts. Projects in deep cover. A night that won't end. He sets up an intercept, daring it to work.

It does. Gage's voice shatters the night.

"He's alive," Maya whispers as if she thinks Gage may hear her. A fire lights in her eyes. His eyes.

Alex is precision and caffeine. Maya is fire and thread. The data leaks out. Slowly. Then all at once.

"It's all here," she says, connecting it to the files they took. Nightfall's shadow looming large.

Alex runs another pass. Techniques. Signatures. Projects spun off, renamed, repackaged. The old dread, sharp and vivid. He shuts it down, powers it up again.

Maya fills the space with paper, with links, her thoughts out loud. "Firm in Seattle. Funds them through crypto. AI patents." She breathes it, believes it. "Three of them. Maybe four."

Alex taps keys, sets an intercept. They watch as the digital world unfolds, messy and vast. They capture code, crack it open, sift through the fragments like junkies.

Their fingers collide on the keyboard. An unspoken dare. Which breaks first? Them or the code?

At 3 AM came the breakthrough.

The speakers crackle. Hiss. Gage's voice.

Alive.

The word is a shock. A blow.

He speaks. Orders given like nothing's changed. His ghost, reanimated. "Final preparations. The island facility. Everything else secondary."

They listen. Silent, stunned, unbelieving.

"Son of a bitch," Alex says. Already pulling up maps, satellite images. "Not just alive. Moving fast."

Maya pushes the limits, hunts for context. For evidence. "What's he building?"

They stare at the screen, each waiting for the other to say what they both know.

It's huge.

It's dangerous.

Alex scrubs his face with his hands. Leans back, then forward, fingers darting across keys. "I want all of it. Every last piece."

"Surveillance networks." Maya lists what they see. "Militia contracts. Two countries at least." Her eyes stay on him, gauging his resolve.

"The island," Alex says. The map floods blue. "What do you think?"

"Think it's big." She clicks through the data, then clicks again. Cross-referencing the way she used to, the way she thought she'd never do again. Shipping manifests. Coordinates. "There," she points. "That's where they're gathering."

The reality, heavy and immense, settles over them. They lean in, closer than they've been since they started this dance.

"Okay." Alex breathes the word. It's a plan, a promise. "We know what we're doing."

His fingers move like he's writing the future. And hers keep pace, writing it too.

There's still much to do.

Chapter Three: The Puppet Master's Trail

Taking the bare minimum, Alex and Maya, move into one of his old safehouse haunts after collecting the key from a still active dead drop. The safehouse is a basement flat in Hoxton.

The room is oppressive. Maya wonders why estate agents use the euphemism "garden flat" and then dismisses the thought. The air is full of static and tension. Coffee cups, some days old, and abandoned takeout boxes tell the story of a siege, of two people dug in and determined to outlast their enemy. Alex and Maya move through the clutter with exhaustion-fuelled urgency, navigating around tangled power cords and conspiracy webs in their pursuit of something they can't quite see but know is there. Maya, at a pin-covered board, hunts with raw intuition, connecting threads like a master weaver. Alex, his gaze on the screen, pursues logic with the precision of a surgeon, peeling back the digital skin to find the truth pulsing beneath. A flurry of transactions appears before his eyes, a sudden pattern emerging like a confession. He's not the endpoint. He's the conduit.

Alex crouches over the keyboard, his fingers a blur. Sharp eyes scan for patterns like a hawk circling prey. He goes over previous data in case he has missed something. Financial data, black and white with cold intent, streams across the monitor. Shell companies and offshore accounts form a shadowy trail, and Alex pursues it with relentless focus. He wipes a hand across his jaw, smearing more than stubble—the stress lines etched deep and permanent. The hum of equipment is the background to his digital symphony, and he's the soloist, leading it with precision.

"Got something," he says but he's talking to himself, a vocal breadcrumb left on the path.

Maya doesn't look up. She's lost in her own labyrinth, pinning articles and photos with the intensity of a detective stitching a case. Energy consumption, venture capital, government contracts—an array of clues that only she can see forming a complete picture. Her green eyes, sharp and unwavering, dart between papers like a predator tracking movement.

"Gage again?" she asks, the words tinged with irony. "Or someone else?"

"Both." He taps a key, and new connections blossom on the screen. His mind races, three steps ahead, thinking, knowing. "Every surveillance deal is followed by fund transfers. He's not the endpoint."

Maya's interest sparks. She moves closer, bringing the scent of coffee and newsprint with her. Her gaze fixes on the monitor, and she inhales sharply as she sees what he sees.

"They think he's clean because the money flows through him. It's perfect," she murmurs, a note of admiration grudgingly admitted. "But who's pulling the strings?"

Alex pulls up more files. "The Architects," he says, reading from encrypted logs. His voice is tight, coiled, an emotional spring about to snap. "He's getting instructions."

Maya shakes her head, incredulous but exhilarated. Her eyes are wide, more alive than they've been in days, weeks. She scans the latest printouts, the lines on her forehead deepening as she processes.

"Damn. He's just the messenger." She pins the new records to the wall, the web growing, expanding like the universe.

"Not just," Alex counters. "He's essential. Without him—" His sentence trails off, unfinished, unimportant. He's already thinking, moving to the next step, and the step after that.

They work like this, side by side but worlds apart. Hers is ink and intuition; his is code and logic. Maya studies each pinned document with fierce intensity, weaving narratives in her mind, making connections no one else would see. Alex dissects emails and ledgers with cool detachment cutting away the lies to reveal the truth. Together, they are a force of nature, elemental and unstoppable.

It comes to him like an unexpected storm. Alex finds the encrypted communications, buried in layers of security. He knows immediately what he's looking at, his fingers stilling over the keyboard, the silence like a held breath.

"This is it," he says, the calm in his voice a lie betrayed by the light in his eyes.

Maya is beside him in an instant, her presence a gravity that pulls his orbit closer. She stares at the screen, her mind assembling possibilities with dizzying speed.

"Can you crack it?" She bites her lip, the challenge exciting her, driving her forward.

"Can a cat climb?" It's an old joke, worn from overuse, but it works, breaking the tension just enough. He dives back into the code, and she watches him, her trust implicit and complete.

The room fades around them, the clutter and chaos forgotten as they focus, laser-like, on this one thing. Time twists, compresses, stretches into an odd sticky goo of seconds and minutes. Maya paces, her hands never still. Alex hardly blinks, every muscle in his body wound and wired. Exhaustion pulls at them, but they shake it off, will it away, refuse to acknowledge its insistent presence.

Then—another pattern, another piece of the puzzle sliding perfectly, inevitably into place. The encryption falls, and the messages are theirs.

"Talk to me," Maya demands, breathless with anticipation.

"References to 'the island,'" Alex says. He feels the thrill of it, the hunt, the moment when the prey is in sight. "'The fortress.'"

Her laughter is a short, sharp exhalation. Triumphant. "The offshore operation. Gage is funnelling everything there."

Alex leans back, the chair creaking a protest. He runs a hand through his hair, an absent-minded gesture that leaves it sticking up, a flag of victory or surrender, he doesn't know which.

"We have them." Maya's voice is a mix of triumph and fatigue, her earlier energy burning out but not quite extinguished. She smiles at him, and it's like sunlight in the dark room.

"Yeah," Alex says, his tone less certain, more guarded. "For now."

She nods, understanding his caution. Their eyes meet, and for a moment, just a moment, the world outside doesn't exist. It's only them and this tangled, beautiful mess they've made. But reality is insistent, an unwelcome guest. It pushes back in, and they return to it with grim determination.

The evidence surrounds them, piles of paper and bytes, physical and digital, the culmination of weeks, months, maybe lifetimes. The implications are vast and terrifying. But Alex and Maya are not easily terrified.

She collapses into a chair, lets her eyes drift closed. "Five minutes," she promises, or maybe she's pleading. "Then we go again."

Alex watches her, his thoughts a swarm of uncertainties. He nods, although she can't see it, and returns to the screen, searching for more. There is always more.

The room looms over them, a constant reminder of what's at stake. Gage. The Architects. The Island. It's there in every pin and paper, in the air they breathe and the static hum that surrounds them. There's no escaping it.

The breakthrough is a beginning, not an end. They know this. Know that the most dangerous part of the story has yet to be written. The blinds are drawn, but Alex and Maya can feel the shadows lengthening outside, the forces massing against them. They've started something that can't be stopped, and now they have to see it through.

They have no choice.

Outside of the blinds and the steps to the pavement, London unfolds above them, sprawling and unconcerned, but the real world is in this basement. Dust motes drift like tiny planets in the slanted light, as though caught in gravity's careless pull. The room, with one window and its blind dimming the inside, echoes with low voices, the rustle of paper, the tapping of keys. Alex and Maya work in sync, two parts of a machine built to tear down other machines. It's safe here, but safety breeds its own kind of madness. They search, and search, and search, until the perimeter closes in. "It's them," Alex says, his voice a triumph of certainty. "It's The Architects."

The basement is perfect, a bunker made for thinkers. Or rats. But they don't think about that. It's shelter, for now, from the storm they know is coming. The walls close in around them with an embrace that is almost welcome. They're lined with printouts and maps, photos and notes. Maya's work. She's marked and pinned and crossed out and highlighted, every inch another step toward the truth, the inevitable. It feels different here. Too easy. Too safe. Alex already knows the security protocols will make him crazy.

"These are today's." Maya hands him the latest printouts, fresh from her research, and for a moment, their fingers touch. A spark. She ignores it, moves to her laptop.

"Anything?" Alex is pacing, restless energy finding no outlet. His mind needs a mission. His body needs movement.

"A few hits. The satellite shots." Her eyes light up, a flash of the hunter. "Take a look."

He scans them, and she sees the exact moment he realises it. His eyes widen, a fraction, a millimetre. But she sees.

"You're kidding," he says. "It's exactly the same. Nothing's changed."

A map, its edges frayed and worn, sits next to the glossy photos. Alex snatches it up, cross-referencing, the gears of his mind turning at high speed. "Coordinates match," he mutters, more to himself than to Maya. "Naval charts show the same landmass."

She smiles. It's not a happy smile. It's satisfied, but there's worry underneath. "If it was abandoned, there's no way they could hide power consumption like that."

He nods, acknowledging her point without voicing agreement. He doesn't need to. The truth is a third person in the room with them. A constant companion. It's a ghost that haunts every sentence they speak.

Alex moves to the table, pushes aside a mess of papers, lays the map flat. "You're right," he says, the admission surprisingly easy. "This is it."

"An island no one's supposed to know exists," Maya says, her voice a mix of incredulity and triumph. "Where do I sign up?"

His expression darkens, a cloud passing over his eyes. He checks the door, the corners, the space between known and unknown. Paranoia. That's the name of his god. And it's a vengeful god. "Gage knows we're close," he says, half warning, half prophecy.

"He thinks we're close," she corrects, ever the optimist. "We don't make a move until we have everything. Then we hit them, hard."

He's silent, watching her, admiring her conviction and hating it at the same time. Hating her calm, her faith, her ability to trust in anything. He looks away, looks back to the map, to the papers, to the million unanswered questions that have no right to remain unanswered.

He draws a breath, steadying himself, focusing. It's his nature to fear. But it's also his nature to know. He needs to know, more than he needs to breathe. And Maya is already pulling him into the maelstrom of discovery, as she always does, as he knew she would.

The hum of a signal jammer breaks the silence, the noise comforting to Alex but grating to Maya's ears. He's lost in another task, his hands busy with wires and circuits, and she watches him, amused, exasperated, resigned.

"They'll know if you shut off the lights," she says. "We'll give ourselves away before they even come looking."

He doesn't answer, the jammer already hidden, already forgotten. His mind moves fast, faster than he can, faster than anyone should.

"The Architects have been doing this for years," he says. "Decades, probably."

"Gage is their front," Maya says, catching up, catching on, catching fire. She paces, her feet moving with her mind, one leading the other, impossible to say which. "We expose him, we expose them."

"Not that easy," Alex warns, forever the caution, the fear, the doubt. "They're ghosts. We need—"

"Proof," she finishes for him, always a step ahead or behind, but always there. "We will have it."

His breath is short, a runner's breath, a panicked, desperate, relentless need to outrun the dark. The dark catches him, every time, but he still runs. Still tries. "No room for error," he insists to her or himself. He's not sure.

She nods, gives him that, lets him have it because she knows he needs it. "Then let's find it."

They dive back in, sinking beneath waves of maps and files and papers and lies. The truth is a life raft, or a noose. Hard to say which.

He finds it, and it feels like salvation. "Equipment deliveries," Alex says, excitement lending his voice a sharp edge. "They never stopped."

Maya looks over his shoulder, and her energy feeds his, like jumper cables on a stalled engine. "Five years," she says, flipping through the papers, absorbing information at a superhuman speed. "They never left."

"This is the operation," he insists, his doubts dissolving, melting away. "This is where they're running everything."

"Offshore," she echoes, confirming, concurring, finishing his thoughts as though they are her own. And maybe they are. "Out of reach. Some bloody little uninhabited rock hidden somewhere off the coast of Norway."

Not out of reach for long, not if Alex has anything to say about it. He has plenty to say. More than anyone can imagine.

Maya is a whirl of movement, capturing printouts, filing folders, a fever of preparation that mirrors Alex's own. "They don't know what's coming," she says, and she almost laughs. But there is too much weight, too much history. There are no laughs, not yet.

They collapse into chairs, moments stolen, rest allowed but never sanctioned. There is no room for rest. No time for it. Alex looks at her, sees the lines under her eyes, the edge of exhaustion, the determination that matches his own. He reaches across, and this time, when their fingers touch, it's deliberate, acknowledged, shared.

The connection is fleeting. The world doesn't allow them more than that.

Back to work. Back to the trenches, the war, the unending siege of information and misinformation, of the story that writes itself as fast as they can read it. Alex finds it, finally, in the encrypted files. The last piece, the final stroke.

Coordinates. He breathes the word like a prayer, like a revelation, like a sin he knows will be forgiven.

She takes the paper from his hand, sees it, believes it, can't quite believe it.

"This is it," Maya says, her voice softer than he's ever heard it.

Alex nods, and the action is both victory and defeat. They have what they came for. And now the danger really begins.

They pack everything, every paper, every file, every breath. They leave the basement behind, trading safety for the unknown.

It's not a trade. It's a surrender.

The lights go off, one by one. The hum of the city is their soundtrack.

There is no turning back.

Chapter Four:
Aberdeen, Scotland

It feels like a dream, like a nightmare, like the moment before waking when everything makes sense but you can't remember why. The air in the warehouse is damp, cold, expectant. The River Dee outside, sluggish and murky, moves with deceptive calm. Their breath is visible, every exhalation a reminder of life, of what they have, of what they stand to lose. They prepare in silence, both knowing what is at stake. It's a suicide mission. But that's never stopped them before.

Alex moves through the shadows, the crates, the disordered space. It's cluttered, disorganised, makeshift. But then, so is the rest of the world. So are their plans. His focus is a knife's edge, slicing through the chaos with precision and care. One piece at a time, one tool, one weapon, one chance.

He checks each item with the same diligence. His movements are efficient, practiced, an echo of a past he can't escape. He won't escape, if he fails. Diving equipment. Communications gear. Surveillance jammers. More guns than either of them know how to use, but not more than they might need.

"How many weapons?" Maya asks, voice soft in the cavernous space. Soft but not uncertain.

"As many as I can carry." Alex's answer is matter-of-fact, free of irony, full of truth. "Grab the EMPs."

"EMPs?" Maya says.

"Electromagnetic pulse devices. In the pile over there," Alex says.

She shakes her head, more gesture than rebuke, then nods at the pile. "How many?"

"As many as you can carry." This time there's the faintest hint of a smile. A shared understanding. A bitter joke with no punchline.

Maya turns to her phone, her contacts, her underground network. This is her weapon. This and her mind and her need to expose the liars and the cowards and the corrupt. A soft war, but not bloodless. Not clean. She paces as she talks, her steps echoing through the cold, damp warehouse. It should feel empty. Instead, it feels full. Full of ghosts and spectres, of the hopes and dreams they are about to kill.

"Ollie will meet us at the dock." She clicks off, businesslike, decisive. It's who she is, who she must be. "Five hours. Maybe less."

Alex looks up, a flash of surprise. "Quick... and amazing seeing he's no longer your editor."

"Money talks," she says, shrugging. "Everything else listens."

His expression turns serious. A warning. A prophecy. A vision of the future, black and white and grim all over. "And money's not the only thing."

"No," she agrees. "But it's the thing that talks first."

There's a silence between them, not awkward but not comfortable. It's too soon for comfort. Always has been. Always will be. They have too much at stake, too much in the air. Comfort is a luxury for people who have already won.

Alex watches her as she works, watches her confidence, her conviction, her certainty that the truth is a thing that matters. He wishes he could share it. Wishes he could take it for his own. It's not who he is. But he keeps it close.

Maya watches him as he checks and rechecks, his meticulousness bordering on obsession. She knows the way he thinks. Knows that his thoughts are not her thoughts, that his way is not her way. She wishes it could be. Wishes she could trade her certainty for his, for even a day.

The gear is almost ready, and the world outside doesn't know what it's in for.

"What's your plan?" Maya asks, not because she doesn't know but because she needs to hear him say it. Needs to know he believes it.

"In and out. Quiet. No traces." He's said it before, he'll say it again. He has to, or he might forget. "We destroy their network. Gage is worthless if they can't connect."

"And if we get caught?"

Alex pauses, his answer slower, more deliberate. "Then we're dead."

She lets the words hang, lets them linger, a spectre in the cold air. Then, "We need proof, Alex. We need to show the world who's really pulling the strings. If we just destroy their operation, another will take its place."

"And if we get caught," he repeats, not letting her off the hook, not letting himself off the hook, "we're dead."

Maya moves closer, every step a commitment. "I didn't think you cared about dying."

"I don't," he says, the words too simple to be a lie. "I care about losing."

"Then we get it all," she insists, stubborn, defiant, unwilling to bend. "We get the evidence. We make them answer for what they've done."

"Once we're on that island," he warns, because it's all he knows how to do, "there's no turning back. These people have resources we can't imagine."

She smiles at him, and the warmth of it, the utter sincerity, disarms him more than any weapon could. "We've done alright so far."

He wants to argue. But he can't. She's right.

She's always right.

CHAPTER FIVE: THE BOAT

OLLIE CALLS BACK IN much less than five hours. He gives directions to where the boat is moored about half a mile from the Aberdeen warehouse.

THE SMALL BOAT IS a piece of junk. A miracle. A prayer. It's just what they need to sail to a fortress island somewhere in the middle of the North Atlantic.

"This is it?" Maya's scepticism is matched by her approval. It's like Alex's plan: small, unnoticeable, impossible to trace.

He inspects it, every inch of it, top to bottom, port to starboard, the naval terms flowing back with uninvited ease. It will hold, he thinks. But he doesn't say it out loud. The universe might hear him.

They load the gear together, side by side, wordlessly efficient, perfectly in sync.

"We travel light," he warns.

"We travel smart," she counters.

Another silence, this one easier, a step closer to the elusive comfort that they can't quite touch.

"Ever handle one of these?" He holds out one of the EMP devices, a small black box, a piece of equipment that looks more complicated than anything has a right to be.

Maya's laugh is a surprise, even to her. "If I say yes, will you call me a liar?"

"Yes," Alex says, all seriousness.

She rolls her eyes, an exaggerated gesture, and it feels like relief. Like exhaling after holding their breath too long. "You better show me, then."

He does. He shows her how the box works, the gear, the ropes, the basics of staying alive when the whole world wants you dead. It's more than he knows how to teach. More than she knows how to learn. But they do it, somehow, because they must.

"Again," she insists, her determination a force of nature, a storm, a gravitational pull that he can't resist.

And he shows her again.

The quayside is emptier now, quieter. The echoes of their preparation fade, leaving behind only the promise of what's to come. The Dee outside is dark, the river's calm belying the urgency of their mission.

"We have to go now." He breaks the silence, his words an imperative, an invocation, a vow.

"Then let's go." She answers, meets his eyes, doesn't flinch, doesn't look away.

The boat sways beneath them, the last of their gear onboard, the last of their plans unresolved.

Alex stands at the helm, Maya beside him, and the water stretches out, indifferent and infinite.

"Once we're on that island," he repeats, because it's all that's left to say.

"I know," she interrupts, her voice steady, strong, certain.

He looks at her, then at the horizon. He can almost see it, in the distance. A ghost of a shape. A phantom. A challenge.

It feels like a dream, like a nightmare, like the moment before waking when everything makes sense but you can't remember why. It feels like the end. And like the beginning.

They set off.

Chapter Six: The Fortress

THE MAPS. THE SHIP. The chance. An obsession and a dare. The small boat takes the waves with stubborn resolve, slapping against the grey sea. It fills with water. They do not bail. Dawn bleeds through the clouds as the island takes shape. Sharp edges, hostile and immense. The pulse between them is alive and ferocious. No words, no time. The shoreline rushes forward. The crash is inevitable. Then they are on it. Rock and surf and escape. They conceal the boat in netting, hands fast, hearts faster. They were never surer.

They leave the beachhead behind, careful but not cautious. Scanning the landscape, looking for ghosts. Closer now, the island is every bit as grim as they expected. Jagged rocks and sparse cover, just enough to lose an enemy, just enough to lose themselves. The air feels sharp in their lungs. Feels good. They climb, doubling back, losing imaginary tails, confident and alive. The fortress looms above them. Black, skeletal, one foot in the grave and the other in a digital future. Old structures flank a new one.

The Cold War corpse repurposed, more dangerous than before.

A ridge. They take it, binoculars up. Maya and Alex scan the compound, watchful, measuring. Motion sensors. Automated turrets. Patrols sweeping the perimeter like clockwork. A testament to paranoia, both their own and the enemy's. Just like the maps. Just like the plans. The netting back at the beach hides their escape, hides their only way off. Not that they're thinking about leaving.

Not yet.

Maya leans into the binoculars. "Automated defences," she whispers. A brush of Alex's arm, but he doesn't move away.

They shift position, closer, more exposed. The sky is grey, promising rain. The fortress is an ominous silhouette against it.

Alex points. "Dead zone. There."

"Standard patrol patterns," Maya says. "Like you thought."

A nod. Like he knew.

They study the defences. Upgraded. High-tech. The harshness of the island surrounds them, hard and unrelenting. They fit right in.

Hours pass, but they feel like minutes.

He checks his watch, checks the patrols.

Then, "Time to move."

Back to cover. Reposition, regroup.

Alex reviews the map of the complex, notes patterns, timings. Calm, precise, cold. Maya reviews her intel, the Final Cipher. Energetic, fierce, single-minded. Their methods different but not so different.

They take the ridge again. This time a different angle, the blind spot in the defences more obvious, the entire island more alive.

"There," Maya says, pointing. "The radar dome. Same as the photos."

She's right. Just like the plans. Just like they knew it would be.

They have the advantage, and it's as sweet as it is dangerous. Alex watches through binoculars. More detail than before. Guards on foot. Three to a team. Each armed. Each deadly.

"Just as predicted." Maya, a thrill in her voice. "We've got this."

Their confidence drives them forward. Or blinds them. It doesn't matter which.

Alex studies the security grid, picks the weak points.

Maya's words are quick, alive with intensity. "They don't know we're here."

"They will." Alex maps their way in, maps their way out. "Less than a mile to the target. Only one dead zone."

Maya gives a knowing look, something old and fiery. "But enough."

"Enough," he agrees. A look of his own, and not just about the target.

Rain threatens but never falls. It doesn't slow them, doesn't stop them. Nothing will. They have their angle, their approach.

Gear is checked. Rechecked.

Back at the ridge, they take position again, ignoring the chill, ignoring the pain, ignoring everything but the objective.

Alex, military focus, methodical.

Maya, unrestrained, obsessive.

The patrols. The patterns. A chance too big to resist.

Their hands cold but sure. Their plans insane but perfect.

Time to move. Again.

No hesitation.

The island, the guards, the facility. Everything where they want it.

And everything against them.

It makes them more alive than they've ever been.

The shoreline, their last lifeline, barely visible. Barely remembered.

Dusk collapses on the island, turning it to shadows, to risk, to one big blind spot. The horizon is fire. Then it is nothing. A tightrope walk. An invitation to fall. To fail. They race against the coming dark, through a maze of grit and determination. Alex and Maya. An old alliance. A dangerous addiction. They move as one. Unrelenting, a streak of persistence against the blackened sky. They reach the fence, relentless, fearless. A small device. A few wires. The motion sensor falls silent. They are ghosts. Unstoppable, unafraid, unconcerned. A cut in the fence. Just big enough. Just in time.

The island becomes a different place, dangerous and alive. The light changes, the temperature drops, the determination does not. Alex and Maya move with certainty and drive. Rain threatens, the guards do not. They reach the perimeter, find their target. No pause, no doubts, just pure skill.

Maya looks at Alex. Knows what he's thinking.

"Nothing we can't handle," she says, all nerve and no fear.

He believes her.

Then, like a magic trick, like something too bold, too insane to pull off, they're inside the fence.

Together.

Maya checks her watch, checks the way ahead. "Thirty seconds," she says. A brush of her hand on his arm. They're exposed. More than just to the guards.

"Go," he replies. His hands are steady, fast.

Then something they didn't expect. A wrinkle. A risk. A sign this might not go as planned.

A patrol. Closer than they thought. Closer than anything should be.

They freeze, instinctive, silent, nerves crackling like power lines. Alex reaches for his gun, old habits alive and loud.

Maya stops him with a look, with a touch.

Her hand on his, urgent. Electric.

He listens, a break in the tension. A break that holds.

The patrol passes. So close they smell the cigarette smoke, hear the radio static. One breath. Another. Then gone.

Time to move.

Maya's the first through the fence, but only by a fraction of a heartbeat. They dash through the dark, toward a maintenance entrance. Toward the truth, toward the risk, toward something larger than they've imagined.

A tight space. They're almost too close to move. Too close to breathe.

Alex picks the lock. It's old, but not easy.

The sound of tumblers, like thunder in the silence.

Maya scans for cameras, looks for the unseen.

"We're clear."

"You're sure?" Alex, like a question, like an answer.

Her voice leaves no doubt. "We are."

The lock pops. A loud sound, a bad omen. It's a race now. Thirty seconds. Maybe less.

He looks at her, their history, their need, the sweat on her lip.

Then they're inside, fast and fluid.

It's a miracle. It's the only way.

A beat, a breath, a sound of disbelief.

Then everything happens at once.

Inside, they barely stop to think. A corridor ahead. The darkness of the island swaps places with the chill of the building. It doesn't slow them.

Shoulders brush, breath mingles, the closeness another risk.

They've done this before, but it's never felt this alive.

Maya presses them forward. "Keep going," she insists.

"Wasn't planning to stop." He smirks, more alive than ever.

Every step a shared obsession, a shared gamble.

Every step a refusal to lose.

They move like they mean it.

They move like they own the place.

They do.

For now.

Inside the facility, inside themselves. Into madness or victory. Into obsession or ruin. Into history, alive and un-solved. Alex and Maya move through corridors as wide as a future, as dim as a past, as uncertain as everything else. They move forward. Always forward. Every turn feels right, feels dangerous. The hum of the building grows louder. Like the heart of a sleeping beast. Like the hearts of two frantic believers. A guard. Close. Closer. Alex, precise as a scalpel, ends the encounter before it starts. Maya watches, breathless, disbelief and admiration in her eyes. Alive.

The guard crumples. Unconscious. Maybe more.

Alex is sure, cold and professional.

"We've got to hide him," Maya says, more surprise in her voice than she wants.

They drag the body into a closet. The risk gives them an edge, gives them life, gives them something to prove.

"Old tricks," Alex says.

"Effective." Maya breathes hard. Watches him harder.

Then back to work. The obsession pushes them deeper into the compound, deeper into the gamble.

Corridors branch like nerves, like chaos. They stay on course, following instinct, following plans, following each other. The air grows cold, the hum of servers more vivid. They know it's real. They know it's right.

"Two floors down." Maya consults her notes, consults their ambition.

He nods. Keeps pace. Keeps closer than before. "Go," he says.

They descend, fast and focused. Their bodies a promise. Their speed a challenge.

"Everything we've seen," Maya says.

"Not what we expected." Alex finishes, because he knows what she means.

"No." She's ahead of him, one step, one idea. "Bigger."

"Different," he counters. The words full of a thrill he can't deny.

"Or the same," Maya pushes back, fierce and sure. "We'll know soon enough."

"Soon," he agrees. "Very soon."

A door looms ahead. Sealed. Unexpected. Like everything else.

Alex hesitates, but only for a second.

"This wasn't in the plans." His voice is sharp, alive.

Maya is already moving. "Doesn't matter."

She pulls out a hacking device, all confidence and intensity.

"Are you—"

"Prepared?" She smirks. "Always."

She attaches the device, wires fast and precise. It works before Alex is sure it should. The seal cracks open, a betrayal and an opportunity.

They look at each other. The risk, the success, the madness.

Then the door.

Then the impossible.

They are the first ones in. Maybe the only ones.

The chamber stretches out, immense and surreal. A digital world turned physical. Turned nightmare. A hybrid of old and new. Servers lined up in brutal harmony. Monitoring stations, wired and wireless, 21st-century relics.

Maya's breath is visible in the cold, in the shock. "What is this?"

"More than we thought."

Wall-to-wall screens. Global feeds. Everything.

"Good thing I came prepared," she says, but the awe and fear shake her voice.

They move in, unable to stop, unable to resist. It's terrifying. It's beautiful.

Surveillance everywhere. Every corner of the world. Street cameras. Satellites. Even private home feeds.

"Nothing safe," Alex says, the implications electric and massive. "Nothing secure."

They stare at the feeds, endless. It takes a minute to process, to absorb.

A minute to breathe.

"I knew it was big," Maya says, incredulous and thrilled. "But this..."

"It's huge." Alex is stunned, determined. "They're decades ahead."

"Centuries," she insists, the words like fire.

Every screen tells a story. They tell a million stories.

A look, a dare.

"Thoughts?" Maya challenges.

He shakes his head. His certainty, his doubt, his need to know more. "Not buried," he says. "Not dead."

A black crystalline structure at the centre. It pulses with light, surreal, unlike anything they've seen.

"What the hell is that?"

Maya steps closer. Mesmerized, hypnotized. "I think we just found what comes after VEGA," she says, voice tight with disbelief, with awe.

The enormity of it all, sinking in. Their lives, their choices, everything.

The Architects.

Nightfall.

Themselves.

So sure. So alive.

Chapter Seven: The Architects Unveiled

They navigate through corridors that could lead anywhere or nowhere. The world closes in, metal and cold, tight as the space between them. Alex and Maya. A duo and a competition. Not ready to win, but ready to risk. Their hearts. Their lives. A door ahead, sealed and secure. Their minds converge, too similar, too stubborn. The system is tight, but they're tighter. A click, a breath, and they're in. The terminal room opens vast and complex, like a secret waiting for confession.

The dim corridors stretch in front of them, a path, a test. It drives them, as relentless as the truth they're chasing. Their steps echo, a whisper, a challenge. They move fast, the chill of the fortress a reminder of what's at stake. Alex and Maya. Opposites, equals.

Their pace is furious, almost reckless. Almost. Each turn is calculated, a risk but not a gamble.

A harsh fluorescent light casts shadows. Their own. Theirs, and no one else's.

For now.

They pass door after door, each one closed, each one another path they might have taken.

If they didn't know exactly where to go.

Maya keeps looking back, her instincts sharp as her need. Her heart like her mind, like the beat of the moment. Fast.

He watches, moves with her. His certainty a match for hers. His will, an even sharper edge.

Then, like the impossible become possible, they're there.

A sealed door. No sound from behind it.

They know better.

They know it's not empty.

He moves with precision, but there's urgency. There's need.

Alex at the keypad. Maya with a watchful eye.

Everything around them could be a trap.

They work in tandem, perfect and volatile. He bypasses security while she scans the shadows, eyes everywhere, senses stretched. Her instincts. Her paranoia. They've kept her alive. They will again.

A pause. Her hand on his shoulder. A signal. A warning.

He keeps going. His faith in her like hers in him. Not perfect, but enough.

His breath visible in the cold. His hands steady. A break, then another, then the final sequence.

The lock gives way. They slip inside.

The scope of it takes their breath.

Their future. Their past.

This is what they're made for.

It's beautiful and terrifying. A technological graveyard come to life. Rows and rows of servers. Physical dossiers. A cavernous room, cold with intention, alive with power. It stretches beyond their expectations. Beyond their imagination.

Beyond what they're ready for.

But they are ready.

They have to be.

Blue LED light glows off their faces. They look at each other, at the ambition around them. This, as much as anything, as much as them.

The hunt. The catch. The endgame.

They move in, fast, hungry.

Maya's eye catches the details. A photographer's eye. A survivor's.

Her boots click on the floor. The rhythm of a story, a song, a war drum.

The cold digs into them, deep as the secret. Deep as their need.

But not deep enough to stop them.

"This is it," Alex says. The truth. An affirmation. He feels it, she sees it. The patterns.

Her focus is fierce, sharp, total. The same drive that keeps them close, keeps them apart.

The same as always.

She scans the monitors, one by one. Too many. Not enough. They fill the room, and her, and them.

Old and new, like their obsession.

Every screen, every rack, every move.

It's all there. Nightfall.

"We've found the nerve centre."

The words slip out, breathless. Excited. Alive.

They feel it sink in. The scale. The risk. The size of what they face.

The size of them.

The light, the cold, the room.

They keep moving. Together. Apart. Closer than they've been in months.

A world alive, electric, waiting.

Their ambition mirrored, doubled, redoubled. It drives them, binds them, blurs them into a single force.

The determination in her steps, in his breath. They dive in, headlong.

The tension, like their history, unsolved.

The scope, like the story, enormous.

Their obsession, like them, alive.

Their next move, like everything, urgent and impossible to resist.

A dive. A leap. Into the core of conspiracy and into each other. Their hands collide on the same files. The same need. Alex and Maya. Mad urgency and frantic grace. Papers and bodies brush as they work through data with breathless speed. Digital. Physical. They fill the space, their energy immense, like the plan they've uncovered. The Architects. The name hits hard, lands between them, unspoken and alive. Their history and chemistry. Raw. Heavy. "Decades," Alex whispers.

Maya nods. Heavier. "More."

They can't believe it.

But they do.

They want more.

The room vibrates with intention, with adrenaline, with them. Data and files, loose sheets, tight figures. They scour the place with a fierce determination, like it might slip away if they stop. Like they might. Their need is reckless, efficient. Their need is each other's.

The conspiracy spreads before them, an open wound. Their history echoes it. Feeds it.

They dive in. Deeper.

No time to breathe, only to act.

To chase.

To catch.

"This was never Gage." Maya says, disbelief and triumph in her voice.

He wants to believe her. He can't. Not yet.

They tear into the documents, the drives, everything in sight.

Maya digs through physical files, traces paper trails, her breath quick. Relentless. She hunts corporate names, ties, evidence. Pulls out more than she imagined, more than even she dared think. Her hands are sure, leaving ink on the pages and on herself.

Alex goes digital, sifting through data with surgical speed. Cracking passwords, breaking codes. A machine built for this. His world narrows to screens, numbers, a conspiracy longer than his life.

"The Architects," he reads aloud, the name hitting him hard. "Decades ahead."

Maya absorbs his words. Keeps moving.

They fill the space, electric and intense, leaving nothing untouched. Not the files. Not the truth. Not each other.

Maya spots photographs of seven people, tech leaders she thought long gone. Their faces burn into her mind, her ambition.

Alex finds payments to Gage. An old dread wraps around his throat. "He's their front man," he says.

A snap. A break. Everything in sync, in rhythm, in need.

Their shoulders brush. Closer.

Maya's voice, steady but fierce. "Then he's just a puppet."

The size of it hits them like a storm.

The size of them.

It fuels their hunger.

They uncover it. Piece by piece, layer by layer, like breathing.

The details sink in, consume them.

A massive plan. A shocking truth.

It writes itself across their faces.

These people, more than just players. An empire. A secret as big as the world.

Alex connects dots faster than thought, like it might tear him apart. He pulls financials, pushes them at Maya. She sees it. She does the same, with folders, with slender hands. Their urgency. Their chemistry. Alive, unsolved.

"We were too close last time," she says, fierce as a challenge.

He feels it, deep. He nods, unresisting.

"They won't bury us again."

The air between them thickens, sparking with shared obsession.

They move in unison, a single force against the weight of history. The weight of their past. Their ambition.

They huddle over a memo. *Project Omniscience*. Everything comes back to them, comes alive.

Surveillance beyond imagination. A plan for total awareness. They see the words but feel more than what's there.

The Architects. The ghost made flesh.

"Gage never ran it," Maya says.

Her voice drives him on, a breath, a fire.

"We're catching up," Alex whispers, need, doubt, certainty.

"Faster than they think."

Their drive uncontained, unstoppable.

And as much about them as it is about the truth.

A pause. A moment that could last forever, or end everything. Maya stands at the main terminal, suspended between risk and history. Between life and a story. "I can destroy it all." The words tremble in the air, and in her. A flash drive. Her finger hovers. Hesitates.

Alex keeps moving, a frantic orbit. The paranoia, the past, the need to keep her safe. "We need to get out." A security alert blinks. A warning. A dare. A choice.

Time stretches. Shortens. Her world narrows to one impossible decision.

"I can take it all back," she says, her voice, her hands, shaking. "Everything."

He feels the room closing in, the pressure like a vice. Like six months ago.

"They'll come after you," Alex warns, his steps too quick to follow. "Harder than before."

Maya's eyes stay on the screen. On the enormity. "I can't let it go."

"You have to." The weight of what they know. Of them. "Or it'll bury us."

Her jaw clenches. Her breath is fire. "No. We bury them."

A second. A century. Time refuses to move, then snaps.

"Damn it, Maya."

He watches her, but it's more. He's caught up in her, in this. The tension fierce, electric, pulsing.

She can't let go.

Neither can he.

Her hand, a choice, a million words unspoken.

"I know what you're thinking." His eyes say more than the words. "I know you."

A stare. A beat. More than just six months apart. "Then you know I can't walk away."

"Not safe."

"Not for them either."

His heart, like her ambition. Fast, unrelenting. "Think of yourself for once."

"For once," she echoes, the words strong, her voice stronger.

A security alert.

The future crashing in.

Now.

An interruption. A shock. But they've felt this before. The certainty. The risk.

The adrenaline.

A shared fear.

The room goes red with warning. With urgency. It makes her choice feel too real, too soon.

"We're exposed." Alex checks the door. Checks her.

Maya scans the data.

Every word. Every byte. Every piece of history.

He sees her fingers shake. Sees the fire behind it. "We have two minutes. Maybe less."

Maya's breath is tight, controlled. "Then I'm not done."

Her urgency, like his. Alive. She works, fast, fierce, unstoppable.

He's frantic, a controlled panic, a jolt of paranoia.

A jolt that says, this time, he might not be wrong.

The tension wraps around them, vivid and loud.

They race to finish. To escape. To stay ahead of what's coming.

Of the truth.

Maya downloads as much as she can, the files, the chance, too huge to leave behind.

Too huge to stay.

The Architects. Gage. Every secret. Every conspiracy. Her heart matches the speed. Her will, just as fast.

She watches Alex. They've been here before. Not like this.

He's a blur, a restless orbit, everything he's never said.

She's still at the terminal, an unbroken promise, a defiance.

"Two minutes."

The urgency snaps like a live wire.

"We need to move."

The data, the threat, the past, the chance. They're both caught up in it, but this time it's more. This time, it's everything.

Her voice. A conviction. "I'm taking it all."

A hesitation. An urgency. He meets her eyes. "And them?"

Her breath catches, a hitch, a dare. "Let them try."

A pause. A wild orbit. It's like nothing they've imagined.

"Get ready to run." He's at her side, a charged rush, an intense focus. "Got the route."

She watches him, the world around them alive and about to explode.

He watches her, waiting for a word, a nod, a sign.

The moment holds, too thin, too sharp.

Then they move.

She makes her final choice, more vivid than before, more alive. The data, the files, the truth.

More.

An electric pace. She runs, a race against time, against doubt, against the past. Against what they know.

Against them.

Alex keeps them on course, a rush, a promise, an escape. Their feet echo on metal grates, their hearts echo even louder.

Maya glances back, at him, at this, at the chance.

The red lights bleed urgency, panic, life.

The data slips into her pocket, into the future, into the open.

They cut through the corridors, fast, too fast.

Maybe not fast enough.

Together.

Chapter Eight: Trojan Horse

A WORDLESS PULSE BEATS under the din of the old fortress. Pounding. They match it, two frenetic lives and one plan. Alex and Maya crouch low, deep in debate and dangerous intent. Every shadow a threat, every whisper a promise. Paranoia. Drive. He shifts his focus again, fear a form of love, both compulsive. Her look says one thing: *We've got this.* His map says another. *A blank cheque.* A splintering hope. She's right. He's sure of it. Until he isn't. Their breathing keeps time, urgent and ferocious, just like before. Just like now. Together until they're not.

A pulse, rapid and clear, underlies their clipped exchange. Alex's eyes keep scanning the shadows, unable to stay on the map or Maya for more than a moment. "No margin for error," he insists, words as tense as his stance. "We hit them before they know what's coming."

Maya studies him, her hands steady, her determination unwavering. "We will." She chews her lip, thoughtful and intense. "But we get one chance at this, Alex. We hit them all." Their planning is sharp, ruthless. So is the friction between them. The urgency. The danger. It makes them who they are.

"Focus on this." He taps the map, a pen more weapon than tool. His eyes, already gone. Already moving. A chase that never ends.

She follows the sound of his breath, quick and controlled. "What aren't you telling me?" Maya demands. "Other than everything." She almost smiles.

Alex doesn't. "I don't like the odds." Her gaze is defiant, charged. "You don't like any odds." A silence full of things unsaid, undone. A heat of its own. Then he tightens his grip, let's go. Shakes his head, his resolve, both hard and desperate.

"Nothing we can't handle," she says, her confidence clear.

It echoes. The past. The plan. The connection and the distrust.

"And everything we can't?" His voice like the tension, a controlled fracture. She waits. For him. He breathes out. Gives in.

"Three jammers, east wing." He says, his words as sharp as the devices they prep. "Two EMPs, server room."

Maya's hands move fast and sure. "Central hub first." Her insistence a fierce comfort. The dynamic they know, rely on.

"No. East wing." He rewrites his map, them, but she's not biting. Not this time. She trusts him, even when he can't. He wants to say it. But doesn't. Instead, he says, "All in, Maya." That's all the warning he gives. All the doubt he allows. "Always."

Her certainty refuses to break. She lets it hang, her focus and ambition more than he can take. Or take away.

"Then don't lose sight," she fires back, and he almost doesn't. For once. Together. Two sets of eyes, two frantic minds. She calls out priorities, he diagrams them into paths. Their plan, improvised. Precise. Ruthless.

"The whole system goes dark," Maya insists, and this time, this once, he agrees.

"Every last piece." His voice is thin and taut. "Including us." She waits. For him.

Doubt swarms like heat and locusts, the halls crawling with intent. The sound, the structure, the two relentless lives. The air, loud with need, too tight to breathe. "Go," his voice, low and furious. They fit the pattern until they don't. A wild card. A long shot. A break in the algorithm. That's when the panic hits. Hers. His. Together. They press on, he draws back. A wire nearly snaps. A gasp nearly breaks. Maya nearly caught. She freezes, this time not fearless, this time just fear. It waits for her to blink. Then nothing. A pause. A chance. Gone.

The corridors feel like they might collapse, burying Alex and Maya, burying their plans. Drones pass overhead, sweeping them in heat and doubt. They keep moving, breathless, focused. Pressed tight against concrete, making their way through the web. The beeps of sensors a dissonant score. They fit the pattern. Until they don't. A drone. Close. Closer. "Maya," Alex whispers, a break in the pattern, a break in his confidence.

Her eyes flare with panic and fire. She freezes, instinct and drive colliding. The sensors warm her cheek. She holds.

"Now," Alex signals, and he's right. Just in time.

They make it through, fast, too fast. Nothing but luck. Luck, and trust, and the fire in her eyes. The corridors feel alive, feel dangerous. Infrared trip lasers crisscross, an unpredictable dance. A time bomb.

"Go." His word, his will, both strong and uncertain. She doesn't wait. Maya fits the pattern, the algorithm, her urgency defying the odds.

"This way." Alex motions, adjusts, a fast and reckless precision.

Her skill pushes them, makes them fast, makes them fearless. They navigate, devices at every checkpoint, their intent like fire.

Jammers on the east wing. EMPs in the server room. The whole system dark. His plan. Their plan. He remembers her look: *all in*. They push forward, heat and panic, determination and strength. He watches. Watches the shadows. Watches Maya. The whole place against them. Except this time, this once, maybe not. Maybe they can do this. His doubt. Her drive. A breath apart. A break apart. Everything apart. A win.

Her skill pushes them, makes them fast, makes them fearless. They navigate, devices at every checkpoint, their intent like fire. They move on instinct, as sure and relentless as they are. Alex adapts, hands signing plans, paranoia a driving force. It pays off. Every time. She follows. Knows when to lead. Every turn, every wire, every close call, Maya a step ahead. Every breath they take feels dangerous, feels right. She feels it too. He knows she does.

The whole place alive. The whole place on them. They push through anyway. They've done it before. Not like this. Alex maps their moves with rapid focus. Her? The rest. Maya calls them, confident. Takes the lead when he can't. They find their angle, slip through, wires and ghosts and ghosts again. This time more. They make it past guards. They make it through security. Fast. Too fast. All in. Together. Until the last break.

Then, silence. The panic in their ears, their chests, an animal beating the bars of its cage. Maya nearly caught, nearly there, nearly finished. "Thirty seconds," she calls, breathless. Sure.

He listens. He believes. Her.

The pattern. The break. The cards, stacked. They play them anyway. They win.

A knot in his stomach, a knot in the plan. "Thirty seconds." Maya's voice, as sure as her hands.

This time. Alex feels the weight of it, the dread, the almost. They are so close. Almost, and nothing else. The air buzzes with intent, red hot and electric. He paces, eyes on a loaded future. Eyes on hers. The slip. The trip. The trigger.

"Freeze!" The shout is loud, like panic, like love. The wire snaps. The circuit blows. A mistake. A million chances. They watch it break, together, apart. It splits the difference. Then it splits everything.

Alex stays on watch, each second a gnawing doubt. Maya's voice, alive with determination, breaks through. "Almost done."

He doesn't hear the uncertainty. He doesn't hear the threat. A crack. A pause. It makes them who they are. It makes them almost. A targeting laser dances near his foot. A blink. A slip. A second too late.

"Freeze!" Alex warns, desperation like panic, vivid and raw. Her knife, his heart, his certainty. All of it in two pieces. Then a noise, low and flat and fatal. It's almost an explosion. It's almost what he expects. It's worse.

The world blares and splits. A facility-wide alarm. A mistake. Her mistake. His. A noise so loud it nearly knocks them off their feet. So loud it almost knocks them back six months. Strobes flicker. The floor shakes. *The plan? Dead.*

Then the shouts. The sound of them caught. Doors slam. Bolts crash.

"Run!" Alex yells, half-anger, half-fear. The panic and the thrill. She moves. They move. Every hall alive with footsteps and urgency. With loss and surprise and disbelief. A strobe catches her eyes. His heart. Her breath. The world, one big red alarm. A live wire. A trap.

They race, like their past, like their future, fast and desperate. Lights flash, vivid and real. They didn't think this far. Not yet. Not now. The complex changes. It traps. They can't stop. Can't breathe. The corridors narrow and tighten, a deadly maze. The panic pushes them, the alarm pulls. Like the past, like them. Just like. They're almost clear. Almost. Steel doors slide. Almost through. Not quite. Maya shoves one open, the force, the fury. Alex makes it. She makes it. Last second. Always. The clatter of metal close behind, always a breath away. The rumble of armed men, loud and closing in.

They reach the catwalk. A final stretch. A second to win or lose it all. The sudden sight stops them. The sudden fear. Alex scans the atrium below, his disbelief vivid. His curse louder. The sound of his betrayal. Not hers.

"Nowhere," he shouts, breathless. "Not yet." He grabs her hand. They make it halfway, halfway gone, halfway done. A live strobe, a dead end. A desperate scramble. The words of two lost lives. Then the lives themselves. Then everything. Surrounded. They fall back, fall close. Maya's clutching her bag, and Alex, and the vanishing chance.

Every guard with a weapon, a bullet, a breath. All of it on them. Together. For now.

There's a loud explosion. "Not us," Alex says, "it's a storm and a big one at that." They look down from the catwalk to see rivers of rainwater flowing below. "Follow me," he shouts as he jumps down into the channel of water.

Maya follows.

Chapter Nine: Eye of the Storm

THE FACILITY ABSORBS THE storm like a living thing, rain coursing through metal veins, thunder crashing through its belly. Lightning bursts, a strobe for Alex and Maya as they sprint. Each flash catches them as they dive into a tunnel as the storm grows fierce. Then a pause, a quiet—two heartbeats. The system flickers. Dies. Comes alive again. Guards shout over the wind, rush to mend the cracks. Maya grabs Alex's arm, urgency and defiance. They keep moving.

Alex pushes ahead, his pulse a machine, his instincts sharp as glass. Maya matches him, step for step. The storm, the threat, the need. It's all there, tightening their focus. He catches her look, fierce, demanding, alive. "We've got this," she insists, and it drives them forward.

The complex throbs with storm. Every lightning strike is a break they can use, a chance to slip the guards, a new angle on their escape. They take it, dive deeper, heedless, confident.

Alex calls the shots, a quick draw on chaos and precision. "There," he says, between cracks of thunder. His eyes flash as he counts off intervals, plans their move like an assault. They slip between half-seen threats, past the guards scrambling for control. His certainty unravels and knits again, a map, a risk, a breath. "Now."

They push hard, weave through it all, the world like a blur. A brush of skin, of risk, then Maya presses ahead, as reckless as him.

An alarm bleeds into the storm, trails behind them. But the storm bleeds back, turns the red warning into nothing more than another heartbeat. It becomes their drum, their break, their live-wire fuse. "Straight through," Maya says.

No margin. No plan. No doubt. Just like before. Just like this.

Alex measures the patrols, times the routes, knows when to sprint and when to freeze. They break from the rhythm, double-back, then go straight into the fray. The only way through is through.

Their hearts slam against the pulse of the complex, their feet pound through its veins. Maya wipes the sweat from her eyes, the determination, the burn. She and Alex brush past a bulkhead, the distance between them razor-thin, the space a dare, a taunt. Every flash of lightning shows them, every roll of thunder hides them. They know the storm can't hold them. They know it can.

A breath, a slip, a sound. Then they're inside, against a wall, a minute, a pause. The guards don't see it coming. The wind, the thunder, their will, all on their side. The hallways shudder. The complex moans, straining against the elements and them.

But Maya's right.

They've got this.

The facility is a fuse box of broken signals, flickering, strobe-bright and dark. They make it into a service tunnel, collapse against the cold steel of the walls, lungs on fire. They see it, they see each other. Only a second, but it expands, stretches, becomes something more.

"Where now?" Maya's breathless, insistent, a challenge and a drive.

"Back through the main corridor," Alex answers. He remembers their last break, their last run. Their last life. It's all he needs to see the route. The plan. Her. He doesn't slow down. "One more minute."

Another breath, another pulse.

She nods, her certainty never more than a second away. "Then we do this."

They take off, urgent, reckless, more alive than ever. Water tracks them. The storm, the guards, the danger. Nothing holds them. They hold each other's pace.

Then:

"Stop." His word like thunder.

It echoes against the steel. A break. A warning. A spark.

Maya doesn't wait. Doesn't hesitate. She knows when to listen, when to trust him, when to hold her breath. She slides into the space between silence and storm, in her element, a natural. The alcove swallows them, shadows dark as the end of everything.

They're on top of each other. The patrol guards pass. The storm doesn't. A single word between them:

"Close."

Her whisper, her need. Their whole world in that moment.

Then lightning cracks open, a flash, a breath, the possibility.

"Wait," he says. "I'm counting the intervals. Guards and the thunder."

The storm feels tight as a fist, close as their lives. His words, their breath, a spark. It's a miracle. It's the only way.

"Three minutes to the next patrol gap." He counts off on his fingers, looks at her, reads her pulse like a novel he knows by heart. "Then we hit the hub."

They wait. They burn. They hold. They have to. It's everything.

Everything.

The patrol moves out of range, the chance expands, too thin and real to last.

Their fingers brush. She doesn't mind. She grabs his hand and the risk and doesn't let go. Not this time. Not like before.

"Then we go," he says.

They're out. They're gone. The storm unravels. But not yet. Not them. They push against the steel and the wind and the world. It pushes back. But not enough. Not yet.

They reach the corridor, stretch out and grab the future. Every step as wide as a chance, a breath, a break. The rain soaks them through, ignites them.

They know they might not make it. They hope they will.

The final sprint, the last leg. The hub, so close. Too far. Too much. Never enough.

They dive in, skin to skin, wrist to wrist, and the storm closes in like an angry fist, like a curse, like a prayer.

Alex holds it all, hard and fast.

Maya holds it all, harder, faster.

They reach it.

"Okay," she says, alive, wild.

A miracle.
The only way.

<hr>

THE STORM BUYS THEM time, a currency they spend at the expense of fear. It slows the island's pulse, but Alex and Maya's?

A live current, a desperate need. They don't waste it. They catch their breath, a sound loud as belief. Security systems flicker. Blind. Deaf. For now. Alex cracks the local panel, his hands fast, urgent. Then a surge. A breach. The complex comes alive, a creature with intent. Doors crash shut like jaws. Maya hacks the system, forcing them open. Then a pause. Then time enough. Barely.

The storm and chaos and their will to win. It fuels them, drives them on.

It keeps them alive.

Alex works the security panel, fingers swift, forceful. The circuits strain against his assault, but the island can't keep up. Not with him. Not yet.

He reads Maya's intent. Reads her heart. All there, burning like a fuse. Like the storm.

"You're done?" she asks, as much a dare as a question.

"Two seconds," he fires back, then proves it.

She sees his need, the history it contains. Then she grabs the thread, the story, and makes it hers. Her tablet connects with a pulse, alive, wide open.

The power strains.

She doesn't.

It's a race against the storm, the complex, their past.

Her fingers and his, urgency against urgency.

"Got it."

Then the surge.

Then the break.

Then the plan gone red, alive with threat and chaos.

The complex shudders, reanimates, a creature with sharp intent.

This time, she does hesitate. But only for a second.

It's all it takes.

For them, it's all they have.

Her world shrinks to the tablet, to Alex, to everything they're after.

She rewrites the system with fire and need. A breathless act of desperation.

The halls go white, then black, then open.

The storm unravels and comes together.

Just like them.

They are drenched, spent, alive.

She knows it.

He knows it.

They dive past the closing doors, grab the chance before it's too late, before it's another six months.

"Close," she says. "Too close."

"No." He draws her back in, defiant and wild and unrelenting. "But it will be."

It's his promise. It's what she wanted.

The final door, it looms, then narrows.

They slip beneath it, slide into the storm's embrace, the fury, the drive.

Everything behind them, almost lost.

Everything ahead, all they need.

Almost.

Then the island breaks.

So do they.

They dive in.

The last corridor. The last sprint. The last breath.

A force they can't escape.

A risk they won't.

They buy the time, take the chance, make it through.

Alive.

"Keep going." Alex pulls Maya forward, his need immense, a creature, a fire. "Keep going."

Her nod, her life, everything on the line.

Her fingers bleed ink, bleed speed, bleed everything they are.

They cross the threshold.

They're not done. Not nearly.

A hallway stretches out, past, present, them.

They own it.

For now.

They push on. A blur of wet clothes, wild eyes, fierce abandon.

Themselves.

A storm's grace, a gamble's defiance, a gambler's belief. They push through with everything and more.

It might not hold them.

It might.

They streak through the bowels of the island, blind to the red warnings, deaf to the roar of pursuit. Their lives, a breathless rush, a need to have this one thing. This time.

Then:

"The restricted area."

Maya's voice, triumphant, breathless, sure.

He hears the fire. He hears more.

It makes the risk worth it.

A new door. Another obstacle. A chance.

The Architects' symbol looms, a sign, a promise, a challenge.

It becomes their compass, their fire, their way through the storm.

They reach for it.

It reaches back.

Another push. Another dive. A thought.

Alex hesitates, then refuses to.

Her fingers. His certainty. The ink. The water. The will.

"Come on." She grabs the future, the risk, his hand. "Come on."

They take it.

They push hard. They lose the chance.

They gain it.

Against the storm. Against time. Against the world.

All in.

A last corridor, a last sprint, the last.

It becomes a war they can't fight, a risk they can't ignore, a history they won't rewrite.

"Now or never." Maya calls it, runs it, lives it. "Now."

The symbol on the door.

Their belief in it, in each other, fierce and unsolved.

Their certainty.

Their doubt.

It narrows. They take it.

"Two more minutes," Alex says. Then louder. "Two more."

Maya won't slow. Won't let him.

"Okay." She pulls them both. She doesn't break.

A slip. A dive. A break.

The last door.

Then it's theirs.

"Now." He says it again, and it catches the wind, catches them, makes them more alive than they ever were.

A breath. A risk. A curse.

A promise.

They reach it, a force, a need.

Alive.

Defiant.

Sure.

The heart of the complex, beating black and infinite. Its pulse is a dark energy, its life a thousand screens showing every secret. A vast chamber. Cold. Colder. OBSIDIAN. Alex and Maya see the crystal core. They see the crystalline truth. Everything else comes later. It takes their breath, and it gives it back, a cycle, a storm. They watch it all, drenched and stunned and complete. It feeds off the weather. It feeds off their disbelief. "Not VEGA," Maya whispers, the words like lightning. "Beyond it."

The Architects, everywhere.

Their reach, a suffocating cloak.

Their presence, global, infinite.

This is what they sought. This is beyond them.

Surveillance streams unroll like prophecy. Every feed, every word, every person. The past and future, merged and tangled, impossible and close. Their dreams and fears, in stark relief, in black and white, and every colour between.

Alex is the first to break.

He moves, alive with disbelief and anger, kinetic and cold.

"Cables." The word hits like an explosion, like his heart. "Cooling systems." He absorbs it all, a thirst and a fire. "We kill it."

Her eyes catch his. Her need catches his. "Then let's," she says. "Before it kills us."

They snap into motion. They are forceful, bold, an ambition unrestrained. A camera in her hand, a gun in his.

They're still shocked. But it won't last. They can't let it.

The storm rages outside, a shared breath, an electric surge.

It powers them, like it powers the room, the risk, the chance.

Alex and Maya circle OBSIDIAN, a black sun, a digital core. Every step unwinds their fear.

Every step writes their plan.

"Did you see the feeds?" Her voice, almost wonder, almost need.

"Like nothing." A breath. An urgency. "Like everything."

She doesn't stop. She won't.

Photos. Evidence.

The light plays on her face. On them. On their disbelief.

They rush through the chamber, through the risk, through their surprise. They know they might not make it. They know they will. They have to.

Alex sees his own reflection. The room reflects it back, a dark brilliance, a cold ambition.

This time, they won't lose.

Maya gets more shots, more secrets, a pulse, a plan.

It mirrors their obsession, their disbelief, the truth.

Maya and Alex push further, faster, more alive.

The heart of it all, and the heart of them.

Surveillance. More than that.

They take it all, it takes them.

A time stamp, an alert, a deployment schedule.

Another strike. Another flood. Another fuse.

Maya feels the ground shift, like lightning in her heart. "72 hours." Her voice is all the history, all the future, all of them. "Global activation."

"Faster than we thought." Alex moves closer, his certainty breaking, then building, then bright as the crystal core. "More dangerous."

The storm's fury bleeds through. It takes everything, and they let it, and they won't let it go. Not this time.

Not again.

The weight of it all. The Architects, The OBSIDIAN. The risk, the pulse, the pull.

They won't walk away. They can't.

The whole complex against them.

Everything they ever wanted.

Everything they never knew.

Too far to stop. Too much to resist.

They catch their breath, catch the fire.

Then Maya is on it, a fury, an ambition, a fire. "Video."

The obsession owns them.

The truth explodes around them.

Alex. Maya. Urgency. Electricity. Need. It rewrites everything. It makes them everything.

"We have this," he says, words rapid as their hearts. "We have it."

Their pace. A machine. A storm. A live wire.

"Okay," she says, like a breath, like a promise, like a shock.

The power surges. OBSIDIAN bright, fierce, terrifying.

Maya stays. It becomes her.

So does Alex.

Her camera is an extension, his heart, their life.

Data streams, endless.

The facility. Their belief. Everything caught in the loop, a fierce and final confession.

A collision.

"Not just global," Alex shouts. "Not just a launch."

The lights bleed out, an urgent pulse, then a desperate black.

His voice, a crack, a live current.

"They're deploying worldwide." He watches the systems as they come, as they go, as they fade. "Not a launch." A disbelief. A knowledge. "A takeover."

She looks at him, their future, their everything, and more.

It makes her breath catch.

It makes his.

The escape. The trap. The light. The black.

It risks everything.

It doesn't stop them.

The storm. OBSIDIAN. The world between them.

It won't stop. They can't.

The core grows, the power's fierce, terrifying. It bleeds them in. It shocks them out.

But they won't.

Alex. Maya.

The control. The need. The pulse.

They push. They grab. They won't let go.

His. Hers. Theirs.

A lightning strike.

A choice.

The data.

The past.

Their belief.

Then a pause.

A risk.

An escape.

They go for it.

They make it.

Or they don't.

It doesn't stop them until they hear a voice relayed over the public address system.

"It's him," Maya says.

Chapter Ten: The Devil's Bargain

Alex narrows his eyes, a hundred possibilities, a hundred questions. "You've been playing both sides," he accuses, words sharp and flat as the collapsing structure.

Gage's smile widens, but his eyes remain cold. "Playing to win," he says, a calm centre in the chaos. The room shakes with renewed fury. The whole world seems to crack, except for Gage, who stands unmoving, unshaken.

Maya catches her breath, stares at him, as if looking through a ghost. "We saw your death certificate." Her voice challenges, but there's a tremor in it, and they all know it.

The storm punches against the walls, demanding to be heard. A shudder rolls through the floor. Alex clenches his jaw, fingers itching for the keyboard, for a resolution. But he can't let this go. "The data," he presses. "The news." Every bit of information they'd gathered, turned on its head. The whole truth, a lie.

"Precisely," Gage answers, voice almost drowned by the noise. The world shrinks around them, metal and thunder. Maya feels the weight of it all, more than she can carry. But she does, with a single, loaded question. "Why?"

A pause, too thin to hold the word, but it does. "You of all people should know," Gage says, his gaze shifting from Maya to Alex. "Dead men stay out of the spotlight."

Another crash, the building taking a breath. Every sound louder than before. The stakes higher than before.

"We've been running on false leads," Alex says, a hint of rage. "You've been playing us."

"I've been buying us time," Gage replies, steady and composed. "From them. From you." His presence is unsettling, like he's cheated life itself.

"You want us to believe you're on our side?" Maya shoots back. Her scepticism fights with something deeper, something more wounded. Her eyes are fierce, but there's doubt there.

A support beam groans under pressure. Sparks fly. Gage doesn't flinch. "Believe what you like," he says, "but the game's bigger than you know."

Alex exchanges a look with Maya, unreadable, a thousand words in a single glance. A fracture that refuses to break.

They're on the same page. Then they're not.

"Trying to get the better of The Architects," Gage explains, casual as rain in London. "They have a tendency to go off-script."

"And you're the director?" Alex retorts, unable to hide his anger.

"I prefer collaborator." Gage's calm exterior refuses to crack, but the building does. A harsh vibration rocks the room. It shakes loose tension, suspicion, truth. Maya fights to stay upright, the world around her tilting, unstable. Her eyes meet Gage's, an old betrayal flashing to life.

"You've been playing both sides," Alex says again, as if repetition could make it real, could make it go away.

"Controlling both sides," Gage corrects, his confidence chilling.

The alarms blend with the thunder, indistinguishable. But they know. The real storm is inside. "You have no idea what they're capable of," he adds, voice an island of calm. "This was never about control. This was about survival."

Alex pauses, the accusation lodged in his throat. Everything they've worked for, collapsing like the room around them.

"Survival?" Maya echoes, sceptical and sharp. "Whose?"

Gage doesn't miss a beat. "Everyone's." He strides toward the core, toward them, every step more certain than the last.

The windows bow inward with the force of the storm, and the structure creaks in protest. A torrent of noise, chaos, conviction.

"You're here for the same reason I am." Gage doesn't shout, but his words are clear. The space shrinks, collapsing, just like their certainty. "They've built something beyond their grasp. They need me to keep it contained."

"Their little death knell?" Maya's sarcasm hits hard. "You think you're the voice of reason?"

"OBSIDIAN is the key to moderating The Architects," Gage says, pointing at the centre of it all, the epicentre, the eye. "It was never about surveillance." He pauses, and for a moment, even the storm seems to hesitate. "Not just about surveillance."

A light flickers, a door slams shut somewhere. But the only thing closing in is the truth.

Alex watches the final command blink at him, every pulse a taunt. A reminder of how close they are. "You want us to just walk away," he accuses, eyes never leaving the screen.

"I want you to think before you destroy it all," Gage counters. "This is bigger than any of us. Including them."

"You really believe that?" Maya presses, an edge to her voice.

"I know it." Gage's conviction wavers, then hardens, then seizes the room. "Let it play out."

Maya swallows, hard. She sees Alex's fingers twitching, hesitating. She sees his doubt, and it breaks her.

"That's your choice," she says, the words low and raw. "To do nothing?"

Gage watches her, then Alex. Calculating, considering, planning. The world collapses, but his faith holds. "It's the only choice that keeps you alive," he says, with a weight that hits everything.

"I'm supposed to take your word?" Alex counters. It would be a shout if it weren't a whisper. It would be anger if it weren't despair.

The power dies, emergency lights taking its place. Red shadows. Blood and lightning.

Maya's breath, Alex's silence, the room's unmaking. It's everything, and not enough.

Gage extends a hand.

Alex stands there, the weight of indecision a living thing. His MI5 past roars into the room, screaming at him to see reason. "Maybe he's right," Alex mutters, his pulse a visible accusation against his skin. "We could control it, build in safeguards."

Maya's eyes burn through him, hotter than the storm. "That's how it always starts," she fires back, voice like an explosion. "Good intentions, small compromises, then suddenly it's the world they want."

The building shudders with violence, matching the fury between them. Ceiling panels crash down like dead convictions, missing them by a breath.

The structure moans, strained under the pressure of the storm and their words. Maya watches Alex, a silent question tearing at her. *Will he choose the mission? Her?* The facility rattles and groans. Every noise screams the answer she doesn't want.

He can see her certainty slip. See her faith shake. It's louder than the storm. "We make this our fight," he insists, his voice raw, an open wound. "Gage says he needs us."

Maya bites her lip, bites the thought, swallows them both. "That's what you want to believe." She feels the floor shift, a treacherous confession.

"No." Alex shouts over the storm, over his doubts, over her conviction. "It's true."

Gage stands there, like a rock in the tide. "We keep this out of their hands. Guide it. Guard it. Do nothing, and you let them win."

The words split the air, a sharp fracture. They sound so clear, so right, so wrong.

The windows shudder, holding back the night. Water pushes through the seams. A dark river bleeds toward them.

Maya backs away from Alex, the space between them as wide as the truth, as tight as the storm. Her determination flares like the lights. They flicker, threaten to fail. She doesn't.

"You're wrong," she says, voice fierce, like always, like never. "Gage. Them. Everyone. It's the same game."

The anger flashes bright, refuses to die.

The lights cut out, dark and cold.

Then the power's back, and so is Alex's uncertainty.

"Christ, Alex," Maya pleads, softer, lost. She wants him to say it, to commit, to choose.

To choose her.

But he's locked in silence. Gage's words are a siren call, and he's a ship, and he's lost.

A deafening crash, and a wall gives way, drenching everything. Water pours like doubt, seeps into the cracks, makes them grow.

"That's exactly how it starts," Maya repeats. "One compromise, then another. They have the power, we have nothing. And you know it."

Alex can't look at her. Can't look away. Her fury, her will, more relentless than the rain.

He can feel the building give. Feel his convictions match it.

The whole room waits for the break.

So does Maya.

They watch him. The storm. The walls. It all bears down, the weight and the fury.

"Alex." Gage speaks with cool authority, clear despite the chaos, cutting through the noise like a scalpel. "This isn't a question of ethics. It's a question of survival."

A bitter laugh. It escapes from Maya before she can catch it. "Some things are worth dying for," she says, a flash of contempt, a flash of pain.

"And living with?" Gage retorts. "The guilt of knowing you caused this?" His composure is unnerving, a stillness against the rising tide. The water keeps coming. His words keep cutting.

"This will be their weapon," Maya insists. "Not yours. Not his."

"Or yours," Gage warns. "Unless you stop them. Join me. Help control the aftermath."

"You're just another piece on their board," Maya says. A loaded glance at Alex. "But they will still be calling the shots."

Gage's gaze fixes on her, then on him. "Is this your decision, Alex? Or hers?"

It's a move. A calculation. A feint.

Maya stiffens, takes the hit. She's a soldier, a thousand battles. But this one's different. This one's personal.

Alex hesitates, each second a nail in the coffin of what they had. "I need to think," he says. The storm claims the words, wraps around them. "I need—"

The floor quakes with fury, shaking their worlds.

Alex's doubt, Gage's presence, Maya's determination.

They all wait to see what breaks first.

It drives them apart. Then it doesn't.

"It's a mistake," Gage tells them, the conviction like stone. "Destroying this is more dangerous than you know."

"Enough." Maya can't bear the distance, the silence, the waiting.

She grabs the tablet, grabs Alex, grabs their past and their future.

"We finish this," she says. "Or it finishes us."

The room sways, all of it on the edge.

Gage stays where he is, his belief stronger than the walls.

"It's bigger than all of you," he says, watching as they turn to flee. "You're going to get yourselves killed."

He watches, as if they might prove him wrong.

Maya fights her own storm, doubts clinging to her, a riptide of emotions. But she pushes through.

"Never thought I'd see you like this," she tells Alex, but the sting is deeper than he knows, deeper than she wants. "Not you. Not this."

The building shakes with new ferocity. Metal groans, crashes, sparks. The air is alive with fear.

And with the thrill they can't deny.

It closes in.

So does she.

He catches up, breathless, sure, broken. "Maybe Gage is right," he tries, hoping for anything. "Maybe it's different."

A mad hope.

But it's all they have.

"We're different." She pulls him toward the hub, urgency spilling out, uncontained. "That's why we do this. Not him."

She meets his eyes.

Not afraid.

Not sure.

Not anything.

They dive forward, more than just two lives, more than just two plans.

"Damn it," Alex swears, at war with himself.

"Let them."

He runs with her.

They almost break.

They almost don't.

Water soaks them, warnings explode around them, all the signs that they're too late.

They take the signs. They take the chance.

The future slams into them, massive and raw and unstoppable.

Maya feels the shift. Feels the break. Feels it in her bones. "It's too late," she gasps, urgent.

Then a force hits them all.

All of them.

The impact hits them all, raw as nerve, bright as flame. It tears through the complex with the force of a supernova destabilising the structure. Gage braces against a console, shock and fear streaking his face. "We're out of time," he shouts. It's more than urgency. It's panic. Alex and Maya feel the blow, feel the end. The core bleeds a fierce light. The whole world blurs. A wounded sun, then darkness. "We still have the option," Gage calls, one last flare before it all collapses. Then nothing but the crack of the structure, the shout of steel and chaos.

The room bucks, frantic and furious. The air is hot with danger and storm. The sound of their doom, alive, raw. The core shines bright, furious, dying. It makes them small. A war cry from the failing structure. Steel screams, glass shatters, they feel it like breath, like blood. Like the heart of the complex. Everything on the brink. The crystal at the centre pulses, burns. OBSIDIAN's light, their chance, their risk. It blinds them.

Then it's dark.

Another tremor. Another collapse. They hear the alarms, the water, the structure breaking.

It drowns their senses.

It's never quiet. It's never still. It's everything, and it's now.

A blur of fire. A blur of light. The story of their lives.

The floor beneath them threatens to give way, but not yet. They lose their balance, gain it. They take the chance, the moment. The end of everything, the end of them. It might be both. The blow is deafening, then not.

Then yes.

Gage watches Alex, still a player, still a chance, still there. "It's not too late," he yells. But it is. It is.

Then it isn't.

The impact drives them apart. Then another throws them together.

"We can still walk away," Gage tries, his words as loud as his eyes.

"We don't have time!" Alex yells back, but it's not enough. It never is.

He watches Maya through the wreckage. She's a story, a fire, a scar.

He reaches.

Steel girders scream.

A thousand words, a thousand thoughts, a thousand memories.

Then they lose sight.

She watches it all come apart. It matches her heart, her life. The betrayal. The fear.

A wall of noise. A world of chaos. She feels it and knows it. It's pain. It's risk. It's real.

"Alex," she hears. But doesn't.

A second is a lifetime, an explosion. A risk and a memory. She fights against the force. She fights to see him. She fights to breathe. A wall of light. A wall of ink. Her life. Her need.

She won't stop. She can't.

Then Alex is there, the world between them.

He sees it come down. Feels the impact.

Knows the choice.

It's hard, loud, the collapse of everything.

"Never thought I'd see you like this," her voice echoes, raw as the collapse.

He reaches.

Then it takes him.

He lets it.

A brutal truth, a sudden chance, a question mark.

Then not.

It's hell. It's heaven. It's home.

A massive crack, the core explodes, but they're alive. They're out. It's more than they expected. It's less.

Alex struggles, fights his way through the wreckage, through the sound, through the doubt.

"I need to—" he almost remembers. But the chaos swallows it, swallows him. The water, the air, the weight of it all. Then he breaks through, not sure if he wants to. Not sure if he should.

Not sure if he does.

Maya dives, refuses to stop, refuses to die. Not like this. Not after everything. It's raw, uncontained. It's the story she writes, the story she bleeds, the story that drowns her. But she won't stop.

The walls shrink, close in. Her world, the past. The words between them, the life between them, the ink and the water.

"I'm out of time," she gasps. "We're out of—"

Then the weight and the crash and the light and the dark.

But she doesn't stop.

She won't.

They are broken, and they are not.

Maya writes herself out. It's harder than she thought.

Ink on the page. Words she never said.

Never had to.

Alex breaks through, finds air, finds sky.

Finds himself.

It's not enough.

It's everything.

But it's not.

Chapter Eleven: Countdown to Oblivion

The alarm's scream, a red spasm. The automated voice, a thousand needles: *Structural failure. Safety breach. Emergency.*

The words pin them down, insistent, everywhere. Repeating like the past. Lightning ruptures. Maya catches up, fast, vivid, like a shock. She grabs Alex's arm, pulling him from the chaos. From himself. A jolt of defiance. "Straight through," she yells. It sounds like then. Like now. Like alive. Alex surges forward, doubles back, meets her pace. Together against the storm. Against everything.

The facility caves around them. Water breaks through ceiling tiles. Sparks fly. The power shorts, flares, leaves them in white blindness. The floor pools with rain and electricity, a lethal brew, but they know it, they know the way, even if it's suicide. Even if it's them.

Alex ducks behind cover, waits, counts, the old rhythms driving him like a hunger. A single breath. A million.

"Go," he shouts, and they bolt from their hiding place, reckless, dangerous. Alex's determination as alive as her fire.

Maya feels it too. She doesn't stop. Can't. Keeps moving, no margin, no plan. Just like him. Just like before. Every instinct alive, visceral. Her heart a live wire. The alarm like a scream she can't forget. The system's voice an echo of the past. Emergency. The end of everything.

Just like before.

Just like now.

They round a corner. The guards, the guns. Too close. "Here!" Alex signals, dropping, rolling, coming up shooting. Fast and lethal, precise. "Back! Cover!" But she's already there, hacking the terminal, holding the door open like she holds their future. It's the only way. It's a risk they've been born to take.

"Now!" she shouts, breathless, alive, a charge.

The building vibrates with collapse, with their heartbeats, their refusal to lose. The old drives and paranoia, everything else buried.

They keep going. They're not dead.

Not yet.

Alex leads her through the narrowing corridors, his tactical mind mapping routes, building contingencies, the way it used to be. A flash. A memory. "This way!" His voice over the chaos, over everything.

She's on his heels, her movements tight and frantic. "How much time?"

"None!" he answers, more truth than he can stand.

He takes another turn, finds cover, reloads. Breathes. Keeps breathing. Keeps alive. "Maya!" he calls, the name almost the past, almost now. She's right behind, eyes fierce, everything she is. A jolt.

"Close!" She yells it, yells life.

They are reckless. They are dangerous. It makes them who they are.

Alex takes the lead. It's a force of habit, a force of will. But she's there. She's not gone.

"Together," she says.

And they are.

The storm hammers the facility, matching the pulse of their feet, their hearts. The power cuts out again, the automated voice their only compass.

System failure. Safety breach.

The words like blood, spilling. The alarm screams red, it's too close, too loud.

So are they.

"Go!" His voice splits the air, decisive and hard.

She sees the look on his face. That old fire. That old fear. "Got it," she replies, fierce, sure.

It's the only way.

A guard. Another. Two.

They don't miss a beat.

They're inside the centre of it all.

Fights through more armed men, sharp bursts of gunfire ricocheting off steel. It makes them faster, surer. Guards fall, everything else still standing. They slip through the closing doors, like they've done before, like they always will.

A controlled explosion of chaos and defiance.

"Can't hold them off!" Her voice a rush, a surge.

"We don't need to!" It's more than escape. It's more than survival.

A door opens. They see it.

A window. A chance.

They're out, in the open, the final stretch. Rain pours in through the fractured ceiling, water up to their ankles. It keeps them sharp. It keeps them alive. It keeps them from being alone. "This is it," Maya shouts, her conviction a battle cry. Her refusal to give in.

The words make him move faster, feel more. They're exposed, a lifetime in the open, together and not. The bullets come hard and close, a furious new wave, a storm all their own. "Left!" he calls. They break into a sprint, the whole facility on them or what's left of it.

Another break. Another chance. Then not.

The fight catches up.

They hit cover, Alex presses hard, blood leaving a mark. Leaving doubt. He swears, grabs his shoulder, pushes the pain back, as deep as his fear, as deep as his anger.

"Alex!" Maya yells, breathless and afraid. It's a sound, a fear, a love, he never thought he'd hear again.

"Keep moving." The words hurt, raw as the wound. "We're running out of time."

They crash through. The main control room swells, an ocean of glass and data, too large, too wide. A breath, and Maya sees her. Waiting, calm. Everything Maya can't be. Doesn't want to be. Dr Voss. Sixty years of steel and certainty. Her calm, her silver crown, towering against chaos. She nods at Alex. At Maya. Like their arrival is nothing more than a shift change. "I've been expecting you," she says. The words coil and strike.

The displays curve around them. Like a trap. Like the truth.

Alex is stunned. Maya's heart drums anger. Shock. The crystal core pulses black, absorbing light and them. They move closer. Like an orbit. They can't stop.

Voss stands unmoved. Her kingdom. Her certainty. Two technicians flank her, focused, rapid, fear growing behind their eyes. She knows Alex's wound, Maya's rage. Her control is a threat. An anchor. A dare.

"Fools," Voss says, her voice filling the chamber, filling them. "Did you think it would be empty?"

"Thought you'd have better exits." Maya doesn't care if she's heard.

Voss smiles. "You think your persistence means any-thing?" She gestures at the screens, the core. "Look." The displays show graphs, systems, commands, light. Then dark. The whole world shakes, but she doesn't.

"OBSIDIAN is self-regulating." She doesn't have to shout. The words find them. "Seventy-two hours to sta-bility. Fully operational."

Voss towers, a monument to what they might become.

She knows them. Their flaws, their strengths. It chills, it consumes.

Maya and Alex, small and defiant, caught in her belief.

"Your arrival is a distraction. OBSIDIAN is inevitable." The storm outside, the rumble inside. All of it like a heart, loud and near. Voss moves toward them, past the two loyal aides. They don't miss a beat, though the room, the world, collapses.

A massive section, unseen, crashes, shakes the entire chamber.

The walls pulse. A strobe of noise and risk.

It makes Voss's calm glow.

The crystal shines like their disbelief.

"We are running out of time," she says, but it doesn't rattle. It only tightens.

"Then shut it down." Alex, his breath a quick suspicion, a stubborn plea.

Voss stands near the core, power flowing into it, through it, through them. She watches the light play on their faces, like an all-seeing god, but colder, fiercer. "We can stop it," she says. "But we won't."

"Humanity's last hope," Voss continues, sure and complete. "We're correcting, saving." Her eyes on Alex. Like she knows him. Knows his wound, knows his hesitation, his fear. "History needs visionaries," she says. "Not cowards."

Maya is sharp, brimming, close to breaking. "History needs unhinged scientists like you, you mean."

"We see the bigger picture," Voss answers, a chill in her voice, a freeze in the air. She pauses, watches them, judges. "Something you've never been able to do."

Maya stares at Voss, raw with disbelief. She feels it slip. Then she doesn't.

Then it's strong. "I should thank you," Voss says, quiet as a scream. "Pawns can be quite useful."

It's a challenge. A stab.

The storm demands its say, battering the foundations.

Alex meets Maya's eyes. Her resolve.

But Voss knows him too well. "Why else let you run free? OBSIDIAN isn't a game of hide and seek. We've let you get this far."

Maya's fire. It should be enough. It must be. But Voss cuts, cool and precise. "We left you the map," she says, surgical, smooth. "You followed it."

Their disbelief. It's not a question. It's not even real.

Not yet.

Voss doesn't flinch, but the building does.

This time, Alex flinches. Maya doesn't.

Voss smiles, and the whole world almost smiles with her. But Maya, but Alex, but them.

They refuse to break.

Maya moves in. Disbelief turns fierce, complete. She pushes through Alex's hesitation, the impossible, the building. The whole world shudders.

"OBSIDIAN is different. Nothing like you imagine." Voss gives ground, gives them more than they can take. "Or are prepared for."

Maya's breath, hot with disbelief. "We know what you're doing."

Voss towers near the core, one woman, immense as her dream. She nods, slow and fierce. "Then why try to stop it?" Her gaze hard and steady. On them. On everything. "Your time would be better spent on survival."

Maya absorbs the words, each one loud as the storm. "We won't need it. Shut it down."

"Humanity needs order." Voss refuses to relent. The truth hurts. "OBSIDIAN is the only way." She stares them down. "Your way leads to chaos." She pauses, confident, in control, almost daring them. "Our way saves everyone."

"You'll fail." Alex joins, sure and defiant, the pain behind him now, the disbelief.

Voss meets him. Every word of hers is ice. Every word of his is heat. The technicians continue to work. The core glows, alive and impossible.

A massive section collapses elsewhere in the building. It rocks the chamber.

It forces them closer.

They don't break.

Not yet.

It forces them closer.

But not Voss.

Her voice rises with the sound, clear and cold. She is more than them. The collapse of their certainty, their disbelief.

"I admire your conviction," Voss says, not quite mocking, almost genuine. "And your consistency." Her faith a gravity. "But you're out of your depth."

A surge, a pause. The lights waver and bleed white into black. Her eyes are endless, merciless. The collapse feels personal, just like her words.

It forces them closer.

But not her.

"Out of time," she finishes, sure and complete.

They won't give in. They won't stop. The collapse, the control room, the heart of everything.

It forces them closer.

The words sting. Out of time. Out of hope. They gnaw at Alex. The lights flicker and taunt. He's lost and sure. He's more than that. Voss sees. Maya fights, hard and unbreaking. She knows his fracture, and it matches hers.

"Not too late," she calls. Her fire. Her need. His need to believe.

"I know," he says but does he believe it? The collapse and the storm. His fear. Her faith. Their world.

"Who watches the watchers?" Maya demands, loud as everything. Louder. Voss is unmoved, is everything. Maya is not.

A crack in Alex's resolve. Maya sees it. "You know how this ends," she shouts, hot, fierce. Her need to push through, and it bleeds and it bleeds. "Who decides?"

"OBSIDIAN," Voss says, "freedom is the illusion. Safety is the reality."

Maya won't stop, her refusal to let it break. "Who decides?" The storm screams, angry and precise, and so does Maya. "You? OBSIDIAN? When everything's gone?" Maya pulls closer, closer, feels the weight of her own disbelief. Feels the weight of her need.

Alex knows that need. He feels it too. He pulls in, tight, an orbit around their fears. Around themselves.

He can't escape.

"We're not gone... not yet," Alex says.

"Hope is an indulgence." Voss's voice a frozen river, a history. "This is what you'll never understand." She never breaks, never questions, but they do. The ceiling cracks with rage, the walls strain with fury. It's more than they can hold. More than they can take.

The rumble. The collapse. The danger. The certainty.

Themselves.

The glass trembles, a cage and a promise. Alex wants to believe. He wants to run. Maya knows him. She knows the fracture. It's nothing. It's everything. "There's still time," she yells.

A warning. A truth. A demand.

Maya won't give up. She hacks the systems, tries to, desperate, defiant. She tries more than that. She tries him.

Voss is more than words. More than the storm. "Order is strength," she says. "This is how the world will survive. With you or without you."

"It's a lie." Alex shouts against the collapse, against himself. "A cage."

"Not a lie," Voss says. "A choice." Her eyes burn, clear and cool, a lighthouse to their shipwreck.

Maya fights it. All of it. She makes her choice.

Maya makes her choice.

But not his.

Her breath comes fast, alive and lost. "Lies we tell ourselves," she says, cutting, burning. The lights cut in and out, like the past, like a fever dream. The sound. The air. It never lets up. She's relentless. She's strong. She's afraid. "Lies they want us to believe."

"Some risks are too great." Voss stands like the end, like the beginning. She stands. "OBSIDIAN protects. OBSIDIAN knows." Her composure is bright and cold.

Alex hesitates. Maya knows. Maya sees.

"He doesn't need you." Maya's shout is an open wound. Her disbelief. His. "We won't do this." It draws them close, and the world shakes, and the world pulls, and the world splits.

Voss watches. She's too calm, and it hurts, and it gnaws, and it breeds doubt. "I'm told you always did believe in miracles, Mr Rennie."

The room shakes, their certainty too thin to hold.

The core brightens. It's the truth. It's a monster.

The facility crumbles with rage, the storm tears through the foundations. Maya calls, Alex doubts, Voss's certainty looms over them. Maya holds it together. Holds them together. Holds them.

Then they fracture.

Maya fights her own fear, fierce, unwilling to let it consume.

But it does.

Then it doesn't.

"Don't think you know us," she says. "Don't think you know him." She cuts the doubt, and the doubt cuts back. She fights. She wins. She loses. She sees him, sees Alex, sees the fracture. The truth of them.

They're caught. Caught and breaking. She breaks through. She breaks him.

"He's not you." It sounds like a truth. It sounds like a prayer. "Not this time." It reaches Alex. It reaches more. "Not too late," she tells him, a crack, a lifeline, a fierce belief. He lets it in. He doesn't. He can't. He does.

It grows. The collapse. The storm. The need.

The doubt.

His faith.

A brutal choice, a truth, a new world. The room collapses, the fracture grows, the fracture narrows.

Voss stands by the core, ice to their flame. "One impulse," she says. "One weak decision. That's all it takes. *And you're the experts.* You know nothing."

It strikes them. Her certainty, their lives. It risks everything, and it won't stop. And it can't.

They run the risk. They run. Voss stands her ground.

"We know more than you think," Alex says, wild and defiant. It sounds like the end. It sounds like the start. It sounds like now. Like the past. Like alive.

The storm hits. The world shakes. They're caught in it, but not alone. Never that. They fight the current, but not each other. Not this time. Not that.

Not that. Until they do.

Chapter Twelve: Rook's Gambit

ALEX AND MAYA SEE the world of Voss collapse. The groan of the facility echoes in the dark. Their doubt grows. So does their risk. So does their defiance. Their worlds apart, narrowing. They believe. They don't. They call each other liars. They call each other fools. It echoes like the structure. "You can't just hand this power over," Maya shouts, fierce to the end. "You can't just let it destroy everything,"

Alex counters. Their fight, relentless, like the world around them. Like their own doubt. Like their own faith. They can't hear the alarms. Only themselves.

The storm in their heads, the storm in their hearts. Another violent tremor hits. Maya stumbles but doesn't fall. "There's a third option."

Alex hears her. He doesn't. He won't.

"Rook 2.0," she explains, fast, alive. She won't stop. "It traps OBSIDIAN in a loop." Alex's expression shifts, doubt turning. But Maya's words are fire. "It will be harmless." She refuses to let go. Another crash. Another risk. Another pause.

"You really think it works?" Alex asks. A disbelief. A belief.

"It will," Maya insists. A defiance. A fire. "It has to." Their chance to win.

Another tremor. Another risk. Another crash. A decision. A chance. Alex demands to know how. Maya details the code, her certainty like the storm. The system won't crash. They won't crash. His doubt. Her belief. He tries to believe. He can't.

Water sprays from pipes, from the sky. Maya doesn't flinch. It's a code. A truth. "It'll stabilise. The patch will work."

It hits him, strong as a wave. He wants to ride it. He wants to believe. "All or nothing?" His voice like the world, breaking, giving.

Her voice like the patch, unbreakable. "This is it, Alex, or we lose it all." A fight. A hope. "Now."

Water sprays from overhead. The world is chaos. So are they. Alex wants to believe. He doesn't. He can't. But he does. Maya knows. "Then let's move," he says. A refusal. A belief.

Their voices are the storm, the truth, the fight. He doubts. He believes. His doubt. Her fire. It's now. A patch. A prayer. A last chance. Another violent shake. "We hit them all." Maya says.

"This is huge," he says.

She calls it. She runs it. It's now. A patch. A prayer. A last chance. They sprint through the collapsing world. It's time to end this.

Their lives, the truth. They run for it. Everything crashes. Everything is risk. The world is a collapse. It's a last chance. It's now. Alex and Maya sprint through the failing structure. Metal falls. Pipes burst. The building groans and threatens. They move past it. Above it. Through it.

"Almost there," she shouts. A false promise. An insane hope. An echo. An electric jolt. It makes them more alive. More them.

"Never thought we'd get this far," he calls.

"Now!" She shouts and it pulls them. It pulls them close. "We have to make it." A belief.

The halls collapse. So does their doubt. The structure and themselves. The doubt and the hope. Obstacle after obstacle. They win. Or they don't. But they run. Pipes burst, trails of fire and water. Support beams fall, trails of sparks. Alex pulls Maya past debris. She helps him bypass panels. A belief. A refusal. Her faith. His hope. A last chance. It's time. The groan of the structure. The fire in their hearts. The world a chaos.

Alex and Maya reach the control room. Everything is madness. Sparking screens. Flashing lights. "Fast!" He shouts it like willing a miracle. She knows it. A patch. A life. They win. Or they don't.

Maya flies across the keys. Alex fights the lockdown. A patch. A life. They win. Or they don't. "Go!" He shouts it like a prayer. She knows it. A last chance.

The core shifts. A belief. An electric jolt. A new chance.

"Do it, then we run." His voice like the storm. It is the storm. She believes. So does he. A patch. A life. They win. Or they don't.

Self-destruct. A run. A life. They win. Or they don't.

Chapter Thirteen: Endgame

Maya's fingers crash against the keyboard, all frantic insistence, beads of sweat on her forehead. Alarms like electric fire. Lights flash like panic, blood-red and constant. The Rook 2.0 patch uploads, slow bars on too many screens. The room shudders with a warning. Alex takes position at the entrance, shooting at the few remaining guards with cold and steady precision. They know the countdown has started. The countdown always starts. "How much longer?" Alex shouts over gunfire. "Almost there," Maya responds. The upload completes. A tone, final and deadly. The facility shudders.

System breach. Initiating containment protocol. Self-destruct in ten minutes.

Their eyes meet, a moment that flashes past fear. Past doubt. She grabs the equipment as he takes out the last guard, blood-bright and final. The look between them says it all, but not enough. Triumph. Then urgency. Then everything else. The room sways, a betrayal and a reminder. The automated voice. The old dread. It tells them to run.

"Maya." Alex breaks the tension. Breaks the doubt. "We win. Or we don't."

The structure vibrates like a mad conductor, a symphony of collapse. Pipes creak, threatening to explode. They move; the urgency never more alive in their bodies. Alex with a pace that barely contains him, Maya with a focus as tight as the countdown.

The floor shakes beneath them. Water sprays. Her breath comes quick, the intensity of their gamble in every step, every move, every brush of their arms. "We have this," Maya says, a promise or a defiance. He takes the lead. She keeps up. She won't let him fall behind. "All in," she echoes, though he hasn't said it yet. Though she knows he will.

Ten minutes becomes nine, becomes a fire, a storm, a chance.

They run.

The building shakes with rage. The countdown plays them like a furious hand. Each move a risk. A collapse. Ten becomes nine becomes now. The building matches their pace. The building wants them. Chunks of ceiling crash. Pipes burst. Alex and Maya keep ahead, just ahead, not ahead. Bulkheads close, massive teeth in the jaw of the complex. They sprint through the narrowing gaps. The world a violence, a chance, an obsession. They turn a corner, and then, and then. Gage. Trapped under a beam. Alex pauses. His doubt. His hesitation. Then he moves to help.

Maya's voice cuts the air, as sharp as the structural shifts. "Alex!"

The old fear, the old need. "We can do this." But his voice shakes.

The countdown is a force they can't stop. An urgency that claims them. But he must try.

Gage's eyes lock onto his, a brutal recognition. "Leave me," Gage gasps. His voice is a rasp, a bleed. "You've done enough damage."

Maya watches the corridor. Watches the countdown. Watches Alex. "We have to go." The floor shakes like it wants them, like it wants them gone.

"Alex!" A warning. A cry.

He fights to lift the beam. Fights his doubts. Fights his guilt. His strength. It shifts, crashes back down. He's not sure if it breaks Gage or him.

Gage's eyes. The certainty. The threat. It's all there. "G o... now..." Then Gage goes limp. A second. A lifetime.

Alex stands frozen. A fracture. A crack. Then Maya's pulling him. A moment. Another collapse. It almost takes them. Almost.

"He's gone." She says it like a truth, but his look, his pain, more than that. The old ghosts, the old fight. He never thought he'd see it like this.

A massive section of ceiling crashes down. Everything they can't hold. A pause, a breath. Everything that almost breaks. "He's gone, Alex." She won't let him look back.

The explosion is a shock. It propels them forward. A risk and a salvation. It drives them. It drives them out. "Now." Her word like the storm. They take it.

Their breath, the countdown. Fast. Loud. Urgent. They know the rhythm. They know it's a trap. The heat, the violence. It makes them more alive. It makes them more.

"He's gone," she says, this time quieter, the words strong enough to drown the storm, the collapse, the everything.

Then they run.

It's everything. It's nothing. It's collapse and betrayal and life. They run through it. They run through all of it. Their escape, the weight of everything. The escape they want. The escape they don't. A brutal choice. A shock. They make it. Or they won't. Water, warnings, smoke. Everything at once. The explosion says run. The explosion says now. It tells them what they know. It makes them what they are. More alive than ever.

Water up to their ankles. Rain streaking their vision. Alex pulls Maya through a gap in the collapsing wall. They fight against the rising flood, against their own breathless pace. Her voice trails behind, loud and full of the future. "Keep going."

"Never stopped," he calls back, though it almost does.

Every corridor. Every door. A new risk, a new fear, a new obsession. They won't lose it this time. They can't. They won't.

Flooded tunnels, sharp turns. "This way," Alex says, his voice barely a gasp. But she trusts him, takes the chance, knows the risk, and runs.

The building is a roar, a tremor. They race through, leaving nothing but the old ghosts, the old betrayals. Service tunnels break. They won't.

Alex boosts Maya through a partially collapsed hatch. She reaches back, her grip a lifeline, a pull, a refusal. "Let's go." Her insistence burns through the storm, the water, the smoke. "Let's finish this."

Security systems crash around them. Turrets shoot blind. The world explodes. They dodge the chaos, a deft escape, a practiced art. "Go," Maya shouts, and he does. Then they do.

A hallway of slamming blast doors. She squeezes through, then he. Then they break past the fear, the fracture, the force.

They hit the docks, adrenaline and defiance. A single boat battered but afloat.

They grab it. They make it. "Last one out," Alex says, a breath, a curse, a promise. A truth.

"Like always," Maya answers, fierce and ragged. She wants it to be true. She needs it to be.

It takes all they have to make it this far. "Help me with this," she insists, and he does, even if he shouldn't. Even if he can't.

But he does.

The air, the smoke, the everything. They fight through it. The fight of their lives. "One boat left," she shouts, half disbelief, half relief.

A punch of hope. A shock of life. It drives them, like always.

Alex hot-wires the engine, fingers as quick as his heart. Quick as hers. Quick as now. Maya provides cover, takes out the last pursuing guards. It feels too close. It feels right.

It feels like them.

The boat roars to life as the facility collapses. A mass of explosion and rain. A violence of sea and escape. They take it, take it all, take it fast.

The sound of their escape, like the storm. Like their belief.

Loud. True. Wild.

The structure breaks. They don't. They know it might catch them, catch up. They know.

But not yet. Not now.

Rain. Violence. Blood in their veins. Fire in their hearts. Everything else is black and light and crash and water. They're in it together.

A series of explosions light the sky as the facility implodes. It sinks like everything else. Like their doubt. Like their past. The future is a world of collapse, of fire, of sea.

It's what they want. It's what they don't. It's everything.

A flash. A breath. A belief.

It makes them more alive. It makes them more.

Maya fires. Alex speeds away, too fast, not fast enough. The rain lashes their faces. They take the chance, like always. They might not. But they do.

It pulls them. Pulls them close.

They collapse in exhaustion, soaked and battered. "Did it work?" Alex asks, voice barely louder than the storm.

Maya nods, but not sure. Never sure. "I think so. But I don't know what happens next."

It sounds like a life. Like the past. Like the start. It sounds like them.

"Then let's find out," he says, reckless as hope. The horizon waits. It holds the risk, the promise. The doubt.

They watch the flames disappear, the dark pulling them in, pulling them apart.

The consequences. The story. The new fight.

All of it alive, all of it them.

All of it yet to be.

Chapter Fourteen: Brave New World

They use the GPS on the boat and arrive safely at a small fishing port on the Norwegian coast. Using the boat as collateral, a fisherman agrees to give them a knockdown price for the boat as well as supplying them with fresh clothes. He agrees to ferry them to Copenhagen. From there, they catch a train. Several changes and countries later, they arrive in Lille.

Then they catch the Eurostar together and anticipate their arrival in London. Through the window, they see Lille flash by with its bright and impossible architecture. Every structure is another structure's ghost and all possible structures' possible ghosts. Maya, pretending, reads an airport thriller. The book jacket features a foreboding font and a lone protagonist in silhouette. Alex watches the scenery watch them back, his eye always to a move that none of their previous moves have ever anticipated. By the time they hit St. Pancras, the platform is deserted, and Alex finally thinks to abandon their disguises.

She texts Alex:

Never thought I'd see the day. She adds a laughing face emoji then adds:

but apparently I'm the master of disguise now.

This is the second laughing text between them since Copenhagen. He knows because he had started a tally of the time between each and uses the same pencil to mark them off.

They keep their distance, staggering their movements, making certain they're never within five paces of each other. Nothing more than two travellers who happen to exit at the same time. She heads for the bus; he catches a cab. She pretends not to notice the double-takes of passing passengers, wonders what the tired commuters see when they scan their worn faces. No doubt the glare of old lights reflected in their disenchanted stares. *Tourists? Lovers? Aliens?*

At the very least, they're discreetly alive, and she's grateful for that. She thinks Alex is in the last cab in line, but then a closer one pulls away, and she knows he's chosen that moment to rely on his tradecraft and slip his position.

He arrives ahead of her, as planned, and watches the door for anyone who might have taken an interest in their arrival. She hesitates on the landing to savour the irony of paranoia and trusting instinct. The long corridor smells of mildew and cigarette ash. A TV echoes a game show or the late afternoon news. They both make sure to forget details on the way up. Forgetting is a more difficult trick than it might seem.

The flat is East London functional: a table, two chairs, a bed, and internet access. A picture on the wall depicts a different wall with the same picture. All surfaces are some variant of the same empty, peeling grey. It smells like all its previous tenants at once, though they're certain to be the first in decades to smell fear on the yellowed wallpaper.

Alex is immediately to work, blinds drawn, wires and adapters pulled from his bag. Maya watches, unwilling to admit she admires his thoroughness. He finishes sweeping the room and sets up a new line. No way they're staying connected to anything for more than the time it takes to plug in, to jack out. By midnight, they have a small arsenal of computers and burner phones on the floor, all cleaned of any recent histories, all conveniently provided by generous retailers who have not yet learned of the recent spike in theft and fraud.

"Professional standards," Maya laughs.

He winces at her definition, unsure if she's referring to the theft, their disguises, or their impossibly low-budget digs. "Cash-only leaves a limited number of options."

She considers the tone. Maybe he's joking; maybe he's sincere. There is no marked difference between the two. "You should see the dives I usually get holed up in," she says. "My last place actually had an in-room Jacuzzi."

"And cameras," he replies.

The mood changes with this one word, becomes more focused, driven. She doesn't have time to weigh that difference. Her fingers are already typing, pulling newsfeeds, watching the familiar crisis she reports as though it's been prewritten. She barely registers his footsteps as he checks the lock again, as he wonders if she notices he's already beginning to doubt their plan.

Their world consists of two small rooms if you count the lavatory as a room, and a planet-wide shut down. They watch news updates in three countries at once and read unconfirmed rumours in fourteen. As expected, technical anomalies and outages on every continent. First banks and hospitals, then airports, air-traffic control. Even phone systems are hit.

"Internet service is also interrupted," reports a BBC anchor. Maya smiles at the oversight. The experts can't explain the system-wide disruptions, can't locate the central failure. They're already stumbling with pre-scripted scenarios and defensive contingency plans. On-air, an official blames unverified code introduced by unidentified foreign agents. At his side, another reassures the public that corrective measures are in place and taking effect.

They barely have to comment. They knew before these spokespeople that recovery protocols would already be online. If these experts had any true expertise, they'd know the same, they'd have known as quickly as Alex and Maya did when they left the island, when they cut the facility's power, when they uploaded the code that redefined OBSIDIAN's parameters, shut it down, threw the whole digital world into chaos.

Still, the governments are quiet, a little too cautious for comfort. Maya's surprised when Alex mutters something to that effect, surprised that she didn't beat him to it.

"It's like they're waiting for the signal," she says. "It's like they're waiting for—"

He cuts her off. "The world to end?"

She gives him a look that says, *precisely*. He's still not convinced. He's still on his feet, pacing. They have barely a moment to breathe between the hurried updates of each global news release, each talking head and analyst with a furrowed brow and little idea of what is actually happening. That Maya has predicted this accurately does not surprise her. That Alex is hesitant to acknowledge her prescience does not surprise her either.

Her laptop nearly collapses from the pressure of her documentation. "I've lost track," she tells him. "Who's being punished, and who are the innocents?"

His reflex is almost to ask the same of her, to measure the depth of her commitment. "One's as good as the other," he says. "There won't be any innocents left when the smoke clears."

"And you," she demands. "Are you still planning on having doubts?"

He rubs his jaw in frustration, unsure if she's being sarcastic, unsure if he knows himself.

They make several hundred cups of instant coffee. It tastes like government-issue and old shoes, and they don't care. Each time one of them starts to falter, another report comes in: a government statement from the UK; failure of redundant systems on a Singapore server; official silence and civilian panic in San Francisco and Moscow.

"The rumours are true," says a harried newscaster from Sydney, adjusting his earpiece. "Everyone in the world is offline." The feed goes black, static and silence. Only a short time later reports reappear slightly more optimistic than before. The media outlets use phrases like: Temporary setback, technicians working round the clock, worst behind us, resources reassigned, damage control. Alex clenches his fist as though that action could steady his anxiety.

"Working exactly as we planned," Maya says. She expects this will need further repetition, but Alex doesn't bite.

He moves to the window, allows himself the slightest of peeks. A red hatchback, the same as ten minutes ago. Two kids with mobile phones with no signal, the same as five minutes ago. Streetlamps on timer, same as... Maya has given up clocking his paranoia. This is a waiting game she's willing to let him win.

She jots notes on a scrap of paper, illegible even to her, even moments after writing them. "You're too worried," she says. "You should know that if anyone could fix it this quickly, it would have been you."

She should know him better by now. That isn't what worries him. It's exactly because someone is fixing it, and exactly because they are fixing it this quickly. He starts to respond but doesn't get the chance.

Her face is backlit by a screen filled with reports of widespread disruption. She remains confident, if slightly uncertain of how much time she has before his relentless security drills overtake them. When he reads about the new glitches and shutdowns, he has to admit it's more than he thought. It's more than even she thought. When he reads about the systems already going back online, he has to admit that his paranoia has not been misplaced. Her headline doesn't make the final story, but her faith in its accuracy remains intact: Someone is helping them along. They both agree this is a story to follow. They both agree this is a story that won't end with a single cycle.

The key to it all is to destroy the key to it all. Their current location, their most recent history, their last alias, and all its forgotten associations. This flat must have been issued directly by MI5, Alex thinks. It's so far underground they need maps and trench coats just to find the door. The rug is brown and unfashionable and holds the secrets of anyone who has ever had secrets. When they cut its threads and find more threads beneath, he knows they're in the right place. If his guess is accurate, no one else knows where the right place is.

"We can go deeper," he insists.

Maya doesn't disagree. Her interest in depth is a little less literal, a little less paranoid. Her interest in what's aboveground is a little more than Alex's. Three days have gone by. "How's the exit plan?" she asks.

He's convinced she won't like the answer. His exit plan, like all plans, assumes nothing is ever certain. It assumes a signal-to-noise ratio higher than any normal person is willing to calculate.

"I take that as a resounding vote of confidence," she mutters, not knowing what she is referring to.

"Confidence," he tells her, "is an unnecessary risk."

She returns to her keyboard and pretends she didn't hear. Her exposé is ready. It's more than ready. It's comprehensive. Maya Dalton, the underdog, the disgraced and unemployed, has taken on the establishment. Her files are exactingly detailed, full of what The Architects tried to erase. An inside look at their operations, their contingency plans, their last six decades of surveillance. OBSIDIAN's true purpose, full disclosure of its potential, a blueprint of its architecture. The real names of the real men and one woman in charge. Not just a smoking gun. It's a smoking armoury. She doubts they'll find enough resources to suppress it all, but she knows they'll make the attempt.

She's scrubbed the metadata, disguised its origins, routed it through every corner of every web. It looks like Alex has taught her a thing or two, even if he's unwilling to teach himself confidence.

"I mean it," he says. "Once you hit send, there's no going back."

It's the same warning he gives every time they're ready to go public. It's a warning she hasn't yet figured out how to heed.

His eye is drawn to her hands, moving in sharp and precise motion, scrubbing, preparing, erasing. It occurs to him she's faster than he is, and he wonders when she picked up that pace. It's the same eye he's turned on everything they thought they knew about the shutdown. One of them has doubts about the speed of the recovery; one of them doesn't.

"And if they trace it?" she asks. "Then what?"

He wants to say nothing. He wants to say everything. He wants to say it doesn't matter as long as they hit the networks first.

She hovers over the keyboard, a little longer than he expects. Then a little less than she expects. It doesn't take much time at all. The server they use is too public for anyone to shut down without backlash, too eager for good stories to sit on it, even when they know how dangerous it is. It has a reputation to maintain, and the anonymous user known as Persephone has been good for its reputation before.

A second thought crosses her mind. Maybe her handle, Persephone, has outlived its usefulness.

Alex holds his breath for so long that Maya considers changing his name to Zeus.

Once the story hits, they're transfixed. It starts slowly, alternative sites and forums, rumours gaining traction. Like a virus spreading, she says. Like wildfire. A cascade effect. Exponential distribution. They each have their own terminology, and they each agree that it's faster than they imagined.

"I'll give you one thing," she concedes. "It was a little like cutting the wrong wire on a bomb."

They watch the traditional networks. They wait for the old guard to catch up, the legacy media to realise they're outpaced. It's not long before they do. A news desk sits empty. They look at each other and realise they've both thought the same thought. Two seconds later, an anchor slides into place, scans notes, receives instructions through his earpiece, goes on-air with nothing more than blind faith in the teleprompter. His words are urgent, direct, and so close to Maya's that even Alex is taken aback.

"Turn that up," he says. She already has.

The usual programming is pre-empted with reports from Parliament, San Jose, Tokyo, Seoul. Each carries the same footage. Each uses the same words. Anonymous documents suggest widespread collusion. Identity and exposure of key conspirators. Unprecedented allegations, confirmed by additional sources. Heads of state refuse to comment. No prior warning. Governments caught unaware. Breathe. Repeat. Live at five.

They work for hours, a field day for field reporters. He paces. She glows. "Looks like someone we know did her homework," Alex says.

It's a rare compliment. She's not sure if she's ever heard it from him before, and she's not sure if she's likely to hear it again. She laps it up and spits it out in one breath. "Looks like someone you know taught me well."

The first day: complete and utter panic. Stocks plunge, bottom out. Her phone rings with text updates: Economic impact? Worse than the shutdown. Political impact? Ten times worse than Watergate. Imprisoned dissidents or dissident journalists? They've stopped asking the question. Tech executives are caught by surprise, by amateur investors, by each other. CEOs get pulled into boardrooms, summoned to shareholders. Their public statements are private failures, panicked cover-ups, more failed evasions.

At the end of the day, Maya considers getting some rest. Alex isn't ready for that, not until he finds out if any of their updates are traceable, if they're all clear.

"I'll take the couch," she says.

"We don't have a couch," he tells her. He lets the rest go unsaid: And if we did, we wouldn't take it.

THE NEXT MORNING AND very little sleep, Alex and Maya emerge from the bedroom. He makes another hundred pots of instant coffee. It tastes worse than the old stuff, and they still don't care. They're up before the markets, the press, the citizens. By noon, all of them have woken to the new reality. They are used to dealing with tech outages. They are not used to dealing with the threat of losing power in the only sense that has ever mattered. For this, they blame the new world order. For this, they are unprepared. A second day, and some recover more quickly than expected, some more slowly. Some do not recover at all. Maya and Alex watch as the world tries to keep up.

Public anger is instant and seething, growing with the same speed as Maya's exposé. By afternoon, spontaneous protests shut down Westminster, Brick Lane, most of the major thoroughfares. Alex stares, wonders if they're looking out their window or watching it live on the feeds. Maya insists there's no difference, and he doesn't have the heart to disagree.

It's not long before the demonstrations go global. Instant rallies across twenty cities. Down with The Architects! Down with the Government! She's been following it all online, hasn't heard the shouts out loud until they drift from the London streets, through the London feeds, through the walls of their less than fashionable underground safehouse. She looks at Alex and he's already unplugged their laptops, already tossed their phones. He's never been this edgy, never this unstrung.

They sit with the lights off and wait for news. For the first time, he wishes he could shut down, go offline, log out. They're both convinced that any minute they'll get found out, that a team of blue-chip enforcers will kick the door down, demand blood and apologies.

Instead, a new report flashes across the muted screen. Maya doesn't know if she believes it. Alex doesn't know if he does either. Some of the key figures have already been apprehended, their lawyers say they were under duress, they're cooperating with the inquiries, they've gone on record with vague confessions. Governments are forced into concessions of their own, promise more transparency than a PR department, stricter oversight, congressional hearings, regulations on the corporations. They're cornered, forced into taking sides. They've been caught with hands in the surveillance jar. No escaping it now, even if they suspect this will be their only story.

The news tickers scroll to the bottom of their screen, to the bottom of their worst fears. Persephone: Exposé Authored by Government Insiders.

"It's happening," Maya says. She doesn't know if she's jubilant or terrified. Maybe both. Maybe it doesn't matter.

They watch until the coffee runs out, until the feeds stop surprising them. Neither of them knows how much time has passed until Alex's final burner vibrates with an encrypted message. It doesn't vibrate for long.

Cleanup initiated, it says. *Time to disappear*. They have not made the time they planned for.

He's all action, no thought, packing the few things they need and the rest of it. This, he tells her, is what it looks like when the public fights back.

She believes him, and she believes in him. It's the first time for both, and she wonders if it will be the last.

They discard anything that might locate them, in space or time. Two laptops left to fry their circuits, two people left to fry their nerves. She notices his hands are no steadier than her own. They're ready. They're gone. This is the least certain he has ever been, and he suspects it's the closest they've ever come to true certainty.

The television is small enough that they can barely see its frown, its immediate distaste. It pre-empts their usual expectations, signals them the old-fashioned way. Both Alex and Maya expect this might be their last flat, their last six channels, their last exclamation points. When a network newscaster is the first thing you see in the morning and the last thing you see before you die, your life has more patterns than you care to admit. It also has more chaos than your detractors can imagine.

This one-room setup has all the hallmarks of another unwanted temporary. It smells like this is the life they've chosen. It's still under the radar, still secure enough, still far from their normal London routine. She thinks it's on the upper floors of a two-level structure. He thinks they should move again, and this time he says so.

"Wait," she argues. "Give it time."

He's uncharacteristically quiet, but she knows he'll argue this out with less patience later. They always do.

She tunes him out the way she tunes out the world, selectively.

The small TV sends its own message, more effectively than a big, widescreen flat screen ever could.

Parliament Investigations Continue. Key Members in Custody. Public Demands Action.

It's been a week since the exposé. Her temporary shock at its spread has become a permanent state of excitement. She's certain it's the same for Alex, though he shows it in less visible ways. When they're apart, she can almost hear his guarded enthusiasm through walls, through distance, through every network they've set up to protect themselves.

Across the airwaves, a few of their old enemies have decided not to speak. Across the airwaves, a few have decided not to speak ever again. Those who are implicated have grown familiar with the phrase no comment. Those who comment have grown familiar with an angrier public. Each night, Maya turns the volume up a notch. Alex never turns the volume down.

By day, the small TV repeats its litany of doubt and denials. She watches with the same reverence and disbelief as before. By night, Alex's absence from this new location is something she tries not to pay too much attention to. She knows his absences are deliberate, protective. She knows her absences are not so different.

She jumps at a soft knock. The sound doesn't frighten her as much as the lack of surprise.

"It's been too long," she says.

"It's been exactly as long as we planned," he replies. "A little longer."

She lets him in and lets herself think, just briefly, that he may have doubts. A week with no updates. No phone calls, no new locations. A week of information at a standstill.

She could go public with this detail alone. Exposé: Suspects In Hiding, Follow Radio Silence! Instead, she does what she's always done. She presses harder, digs deeper, gets to the end of what there is to uncover. His unexpected appearance is both a new surprise and an old standard. "I didn't think you'd—"

"I don't want to leave you."

She tries to figure out how this one ambiguous line could be the truth, a threat, an alibi. His silence is too open to too many interpretations. The only real evidence she has is that he means exactly what he says.

"Alone," he adds, just so she won't get the wrong idea. She thinks he means it as a concession. She takes it as a last warning.

With Alex, she never knows what she'll be faced with until it's at her doorstep. She never knows what she'll face alone.

His pace has quickened since they last met, since she last caught the real-world effects of their exposé. Three of The Architects have been taken into custody. She's both pleased and troubled by how few of them remain at large. Anonymous Story Reposted Worldwide. Attempts To Suppress Fail. It's already translated into twenty-seven languages, some that Alex never even thought to encode, and downloaded millions of times. In case they get traced, she already has a cover story: Subversive Author Unable To Keep Up With Demand. In case they don't get traced, she has no cover story at all.

"It's working," she says. "And it's a much bigger story than I thought."

She expects a reply. None comes. She doesn't know if this is good or bad, a positive or negative charge.

"It's the same story we both thought," Alex says.

His delivery is slightly delayed, like a newsfeed interrupted. She watches his progress with all the eagerness and anticipation of a late-breaking update. Then she realises he's not giving an inch, and he's not taking his coat off.

"You're serious?" she asks.

"I'm alive."

"You want to disappear."

"It's what we do."

"You think I'll miss you."

"Yes." There's not much room for doubt.

He's more rushed than last time, less steady, more certain. He's more certain this won't be like last time. He's more certain this will be exactly like last time. Maya doesn't have to guess which possibility he's worried about.

They work quickly and with precision, the old rhythm of doubt and resolve, a seasoned team of panicked professionals. He tells her this could be the big one. He tells her this could be the last one. She wants to tell him she's not sure if it's the story they're chasing, or the story that's chasing them. She doesn't. Instead, she lets him chase it for her. He's packed their few possessions in record time. He's thrown his nerves into the same suitcase.

"Alex."

He looks up, knows what's coming. He knows how far she might run.

"Alex," she repeats. "Do you think there's ever an end?"

"To us?"

"To the story."

He doesn't answer. His silence is its own kind of truth.

He sets two passports on the table, like an ultimatum, like a lifeline, like a variation on the same theme they've been playing forever. It means he wants to go. It means he wants her to come with him. Two train tickets. They're punched with destinations he hasn't even told her about yet. It means he's thought ahead. It means she's thought the same.

She's quiet, unsure, frustrated. She's uncharacteristically Maya. He thinks this might be their final surprise. He knows it will not be.

He wonders if this is the one time she'll choose not to follow. He wonders if she'll wait until it's too late to reappear. He wonders if there will be a return. He never used to wonder.

It's what we do, he told her. But he knows that it may be less what they do, and more what they are.

They're halfway down the corridor, two-quarters out the door. They've left all evidence of themselves, just like they always leave it. More permanent than they want it to be. Less permanent than the establishment needs it to be. Maya suddenly thinks it might not matter, suddenly thinks she knows why.

At the bottom of the stairwell, she slows. She stops. She knows Alex won't wait. She wonders if Alex will wait. He's both more and less predictable than the government agencies he used to ghostwrite for. She turns, runs back, grabs the final burner phone on the table. It has the last message she'll ever get from him. The first message she'll get for herself.

No more messages. Only choices.

It's a line she's read before. She just didn't expect to read it again, not like this, not in this context. This time, the meaning is clearer. It's still redacted, and she has the perfect words to fill in the gaps.

She drops the phone into the microwave oven, watches it incinerate, watches it short out, knows the signal is clear. It occurs to her that maybe she needs him to disappear.

When Alex said, "It's what we do," he didn't mean the stories, the risks, the exposés. When Alex said, "It's what we do," he meant her.

She catches up with the past. She catches up with Alex.

"Ready?" he asks, waiting longer than expected. He's still at the door, but now the door is further away.

Maya is further away, too, and this makes the distance between them shorter than it has ever been.

She nods. She runs. She's never been this sure before. Never this sure that she'll be unsure again.

EPILOGUE: THE ROAD AHEAD

London whispers through the thin walls. A couple argues downstairs, drunken shouts muffled by rain. Sirens flare, then fade. On the desk, her laptop casts Maya's shadow long and lean against the bare floor. The flat feels emptier without his paranoia bristling in the corners. She stares at the screen, blinking at the bright lines of text. They fracture in her eyes like afterimages, too much to focus on at once. Too many connections. The fingers of her right hand flex around a pen, gripping and releasing in a steady rhythm. Sharp pain where her teeth worry her lip. She should stop, breathe, regroup. Her hand reaches to close the laptop, but it lands on something else. The encrypted device. A familiar heaviness in her palm. When it pings, the sound drills through her skull, dredges him up from the quiet.

Weeks have passed since she last heard from Alex. Weeks since the island, the chaos, the impossible risk. Since they burned everything to the ground and scattered like ashes. She picks up the device and puts it back down. Forces herself to look at the laptop again, at the lines of data that won't hold still in her mind. The Architects. OBSIDIAN. Her exposé had shaken their foundations, made waves she couldn't stop even if she wanted to. The world keeps changing, spinning around her while she sits, alone, in this cold flat. She brushes a stray hair back, tucks it behind her ear. Her eyes blur, and she blinks fast to clear them. Outside, rain bleeds into the dark. She glances at the device, feels it draw her in, like gravity.

Three in the morning. Her vision clouds with exhaustion, every word on the screen double. Triple. The glow etches shadows into her skin, thin lines of light and dark that shift when she moves. Every few seconds she switches windows, cross-checking, fact-checking. Updating. Threads of information bind her wrists and won't let go. Her lip is raw where she's bitten it. The pen clatters to the floor. She stares at it. Then the ping comes again, electric in the quiet, and she almost shoves the laptop aside.

The encrypted device. Secure, anonymous. The ringtone unmistakable, and she knows exactly who it's from. Alex, speaking across silence. Finally. It's what she's been hoping for and dreading, that sudden crack in the distance between them. She feels her pulse in her throat, quick and hot. This is what he does—vanishes, reappears, sets everything spinning again. Her hand hovers above the device, paralysed. Weeks of nothing, and then this. Is he reaching out or letting go?

She breathes deep, grounding herself. The sound of her heartbeat slows. Her fingers close around the device. Smooth metal against her skin. Heavy. Familiar. One breath, then another. She holds it tight, waiting for the ping to come again, for her courage to catch up. She's not ready, but she activates it anyway.

The screen lights up, urgent.

No more messages. Only choices.

Five words. Five blows. She reads them once, twice, a dozen times, but they stay the same. The last of him on this small square of light, taunting her with what he's not saying. A challenge. An ending. Her mind spirals, thoughts colliding in a rush.

She closes her eyes, her fingers tightening around the device. She can't lose her grip, can't let it slip away. Alex, always one step ahead, one step apart. She imagines his eyes, sharp and cool, as he wrote this. Her jaw sets. Her hands move before she's thought it through, hitting buttons, confirming what she already knows. It's his farewell, his final word. Her throat constricts, tight and painful. She swallows, pushes through the tangle of feelings she can't name.

Her eyes open, and she reads the message again. The shock ebbs, replaced by something else. Understanding, creeping in at the edges. Resolve, chasing close behind. It's a break and a gift, a dare and a promise. It's everything she expected and nothing she was ready for. She's been alone before, always, even with him beside her. His challenge. His faith in her. She thinks of the past weeks, the noise and danger, and now the quiet. Her body remembers, one muscle at a time. Her head bows slightly, a nod to the inevitability of it all.

Alex. Always Alex. She lets out a breath she didn't know she was holding. One beat, then another, and she's back in control, the message glowing in front of her. He trusts her to find her own way. She must. She will.

The flat looms around her, as if the room has grown large and she has shrunk in its centre. She drifts to the window, the device cool in her hand. Rain slides down the glass, and she watches it until the drops become bright paths of light, cutting across the skyline like ghostly power lines. The world outside, huge and humming. The device still warm from his message. She thinks about deleting it, wipes that thought away as quickly as it comes. She can never let go. Except, she must. The weight of it all is less than she expected, floats through her on a sharp breath.

Her fingers wrap tight around the device, and she imagines a million lives unfolding through the dark. Stories she helped set loose. Her forehead presses against the glass, and the city bends and shivers through the wet pane. London, distant but alive. Some buildings glow with stubborn light, refusing to yield to the late hour or the storm. She closes her eyes and sees his words, stark against the dark. Her mind pulls back to him, to choices, to all that came before. *Can she? Will she?* The questions swell until she feels they might burst through her skin.

Maya draws back, looks at the lights again. The city sparks in her vision, white-hot. There are other choices. Other connections. A digital web spun so wide that she's caught in its strands, unsure which way to turn. She's let herself get tangled up in it before. Not this time. Her reflection meets her gaze in the window, shadowed but fierce. She watches herself hold the device between both hands, its hard edges digging into her palm. This time, she will do the catching.

Time stretches. The rain streaks sideways. A helicopter, a plane, something loud cuts through the sky, quick and sharp. Her heart follows the sound, races with it until the noise fades. Until the quiet wraps back around her, soft and heavy, like a coat that's grown too large. The recent chaos has the edges of a dream. Unreal. The cramped space of the flat magnifies her aloneness, the depth of her isolation after the island. But it's also what makes everything feel possible. The room is so small, but her choices expand to enlarge it. It also feels empty... so empty that she can start again. So bright that her eyes ache, just a little, from the sight.

She shifts her gaze to the device, turns it over and over. Alex and his cryptic riddles. Even now, he finds a way to pull the strings. But this time, the last time, the only strings are the ones she makes. She pictures the world outside, limitless, but her vision tunnels down to the small object in her hands, as if it's the only thing left in the universe.

No more messages. Only choices. The simplicity of it takes her breath away. She sets the device on the windowsill, keeps one hand on it, as if afraid it might leap away. Her fingers tremble with the weight of the decision, her certainty colliding with something much harder.

She's not that person, is she? She never was, but she's learning. Trust, more fragile than truth. Letting go, more impossible than any headline she's written. The message sits there, a faint light under her palm. It's not Alex she's deleting. Not really. It's the way she let him steer the direction of things. It's the way she steered them herself. Her thumb hesitates, then presses with a confidence she almost believes. Confirmation. A dark screen. A new beginning.

She watches it, feeling the past weeks rush away, pulled by the same gravity that has always drawn her forward. She lifts the device, places it back on the desk. Walks to the window and leans against it, forehead to glass, arm extended like a question. The buildings reach toward her, points of light cutting through the dark. The rain makes the skyline quiver. Her silhouette is thin, but it's only that: a silhouette. She knows she is more than that. She straightens her posture. This new world might be brave, or it might not. But it is hers, and that will have to be enough.

THE END

A Request

I sincerely hope you enjoyed reading this book as much as I enjoyed writing it. If you did, I would greatly appreciate a short review on the platform where you bought the book. Reviews are crucial for any author, and even just a line or two can make a huge difference.

ABOUT STEPHEN BENTLEY

Stephen Bentley is an award-winning author. Of his first true crime novel, UNDERCOVER, screenwriter and novelist, writer of 'Julie' BBC Drama, Rob Gittins, said, "The fascinating and extraordinary inside story from the man who was actually there."

Of his later fiction works, British crime author, Pat MacDonald said, "I knew when I read the author's first book 'Undercover: Operation Julie' although non-fiction that he could make the transition to writing fiction; I was right. He has an ease of language that lends itself to storytelling; he tells it as if he was there in the plot and why shouldn't he having been an undercover cop in the real world? Not that Steve Regan is meant to be him, but having the experience means he can do whatever he wants with his fictional characters, and they will always be believable."

Like some other authors, his life experience is broad and unconventional. He spent 30 years in the legal system, first as a detective for 15 years then as barrister plying his trade as "a wig for hire" in London and the English provinces.

He was a pioneering undercover cop on Operation Julie and as a barrister defended in trials involving murder, rape, drug importation, other serious crimes and defended soldiers at courts-martial.

He worked in a warehouse. Rode a big motorbike as a London courier. He drove big articulated trucks and taught how to drive them. He also worked as a hospital porter twice. He drove chilled delivery vans in London in the 1990s to fund his law degree and bar school studies. He spent the last two years of his working life driving plant and operating heavy filtration machinery for Europe's largest water company. His work mates soon recognised his advocacy skills and elected him as their shop steward.

He has now written over twenty books. Two of them have been optioned and in development; one as a TV drama series, and one as a drama doc.

His wife is a better person than him in all regards and is a source of support in his goal of entertaining readers. She has also made him a better person.

For new releases and news about the Operation Julie TV series/documentary, you may wish to subscribe to Stephen's newsletter here. Or use the QR code below:

Stephen now has a Ko-Fi page where members have exclusive access to (1) serialisation of all his future releases before publication in all his pen names, (2) a free digital copy of those releases, and (3) exclusive discounts on merch and bespoke products. Use that link or the QR code below to access the page.

Stephen's Ko-Fi Page

Now a multi-genre author, Stephen also writes cozy mysteries in the pen name of KJ Cornwall.

You can listen to Stephen talking about his Operation Julie undercover days on the BBC Radio 4 Life Changing programme/podcast available 24/7 worldwide on BBC

Sounds. And on the same platform, he also contributes to Acid Dream: The Great LSD Plot.

ALSO BY STEPHEN BENTLEY

You can find all of Stephen Bentley's books here on his website where his catalogue is kept updated.
They include his bestselling true crime books and crime fiction series including:
The Steve Regan Undercover Cop Thrillers
The Detective Matt Deal Thrillers
L.A. Cyber Noir Mysteries
The Last Message Trilogy
You may also find his books here at Booklinker including those written in a pen name. Alternatively, use the QR code below to access the same page.